Poor Folk

DOVER · THRIFT · EDITIONS

Poor Folk

FYODOR DOSTOYEVSKY

Translated by
Constance Garnett

DOVER PUBLICATIONS, INC.
Mineola, New York

DOVER THRIFT EDITIONS

GENERAL EDITOR: MARY CAROLYN WALDREP
EDITOR OF THIS VOLUME: SUSAN L. RATTINER

Bibliographical Note

This Dover edition, first published in 2007, is an unabridged republication of the Constance Garnett translation of the work, as originally published in the collection *The Gambler and Other Stories* by W. Heinemann, London, in 1914. A new introductory Note has been specially prepared for the present edition.

Library of Congress Cataloging-in-Publication Data

Dostoyevsky, Fyodor, 1821–1881.
　　[Bednye liudi. English]
　　Poor folk / Fyodor Dostoyevsky ; translated by Constance Garnett.
　　　　p. cm. (Dover thrift editions)
　　Originally published as part of the collection The gambler and other stories: London: Heinemann, 1914. With new introd.
　　ISBN 0-486-45661-7 (pbk.)
　　　1. Garnett, Constance Black, 1862–1946. 2. Dostoyevsky, Fyodor, 1821–1881. Gambler and other stories. I. Title. II. Series.

PG3326.B4 2007

2006047014

Manufactured in the United States of America
Dover Publications, Inc., 31 East 2nd Street, Mineola, N.Y. 11501

Note

FYODOR DOSTOYEVSKY (1821–1881) was born and raised in Moscow, where he was educated before attending the School of Military Engineers in St. Petersburg. After three years in the army, Dostoyevsky resigned to devote himself to writing. In 1843, he published his first work, a translation of Balzac's novel *Eugénie Grandet*. His first novel, *Poor Folk,* written in 1845, brought him exuberant critical praise, most notably from Vissarion Belinsky, a leading critic of the day, and fame followed virtually overnight. Proclaimed "the next Gogol," Dostoyevsky was hailed as a powerful new talent in Russian literature. Having gained instant celebrity at the age of twenty-four, Dostoyevsky proceeded to publish ten novels and short stories within the next five years. However, his subsequent works did not enjoy the same popular success, the fault of largely unrealistic expectations from both critics and the public.

In 1849, Dostoyevsky was arrested and imprisoned in the Petropavlovsk Fortress in St. Petersburg for his participation in a French utopian socialist group led by Petrashevsky, a rich political dilettante. In addition to reviewing political books banned by the government, the Petrashevsky circle also debated pertinent social reform issues of the day. Along with several other liberal-minded intellectuals, Dostoyevsky was tried for treasonous activities and sentenced to death, a decree that was later changed to four years of hard labor in a Siberian prison followed by four more years as a soldier in the ranks. However, this commuted sentence was not revealed until a stunningly malicious joke had been played out on the group; Dostoyevsky and his cohorts were actually standing before the firing squad and were told the truth at the last moment: that this was just a mock execution. He was released from prison in 1854, and he did not return to St. Petersburg until 1859. His time in the penal colony did much to shape the author's political and religious beliefs, bringing him away from his youthful liberal leanings and toward the orthodoxy of the Russian church; it did much as well to exacerbate the epilepsy that would plague him for the rest of his life.

Written in epistolary form, in which letters of correspondence take the place of narration and dialogue, *Poor Folk* tells the story of a bleak and hopeless love between a clerk and a poor young seamstress. Depicting the tragedies of everyday life, this early fictional work contains a remarkably vivid characterization for a novel composed solely of letters between characters. This natural ability to connect his readers emotionally to his characters has become one of the hallmarks of Dostoyevsky's skillful writing style. Although the powerful appeal of *Poor Folk* is often overshadowed by the sumptuous success of his later masterpieces such as *Crime and Punishment* (1866), *The Idiot* (1868), and *The Brothers Karamazov* (1880), the author's forte in dramatizing the many social and moral problems confronting mankind is conveyed well here.

POOR FOLK

A NOVEL

Ah, these story tellers! If only they would write anything useful, pleasant, soothing, but they will unearth all sorts of hidden things! ... I would prohibit their writing! Why, it is beyond everything; you read ... and you can't help thinking—and then all sorts of foolishness comes into your head; I would really prohibit their writing; I would simply prohibit it altogether.

PRINCE V. F. ODOEVSKY.

April 8.

MY PRECIOUS VARVARA ALEXYEVNA,

I was happy yesterday, immensely happy, impossibly happy! For once in your life, you obstinate person, you obeyed me. At eight o'clock in the evening I woke up (you know, little mother, that I love a little nap of an hour or two when my work is over). I got out a candle, I got paper ready, was mending a pen when suddenly I chanced to raise my eyes—upon my word it set my heart dancing! So you understood what I wanted, what was my heart's desire! I saw a tiny corner of your window-curtain twitched back and caught against the pot of balsams, just exactly as I hinted that day. Then I fancied I caught a glimpse of your little face at the window, that you were looking at me from your little room, that you were thinking of me. And how vexed I was, my darling, that I could not make out your charming little face distinctly! There was a time when we, too, could see clearly, dearie. It is poor fun being old, my own! Nowadays everything seems sort of spotty before my eyes; if one works a little in the evening, writes something, one's eyes are so red and tearful in the morning that one is really ashamed before strangers. In my imagination, though, your smile was beaming, my little angel, your kind friendly little smile; and I had just the same sensation in my heart as when I kissed you, Varinka, do you remember, little angel? Do you know, my darling, I even fancied that you shook your little finger at me? Did you, you naughty girl? You must be sure to describe all that fully in your letter.

Come, what do you think of our little plan about your curtain, Varinka? It is delightful, isn't it? Whether I am sitting at work, or lying down for a nap, or waking up, I know that you are thinking about me over there, you are remembering me and that you are well and cheerful. You drop the curtain—it means "Good-bye, Makar Alexyevitch, it's bedtime!" You draw it up—"Good morning, Makar Alexyevitch, how have you slept or are you quite well, Makar Alexyevitch? As for me, thank God, I am well and all right!" You see, my darling, what a clever idea; there is no need of letters! It's cunning, isn't it? And you know it was my idea. What do you say to me now, Varvara Alexyevna?

I beg to inform you, Varvara Alexyevna, my dear, that I slept last night excellently, contrary to my expectations, at which I am very much pleased; though in new lodgings, after moving, it is always difficult to sleep; there is always some little thing amiss.

I got up this morning as gay as a lark! What a fine morning it was, my darling! Our window was opened; the sun shone so brightly; the birds were chirping; the air was full of the scents of spring and all nature seemed coming back to life—and everything else was to correspond; everything was right, to fit the spring. I even had rather pleasant dreams to-day, and my dreams were all of you, Varinka. I compared you with a bird of the air created for the delight of men and the adornment of nature. Then I thought, Varinka, that we men, living in care and anxiety, must envy the careless and innocent happiness of the birds of the air—and more of the same sort, like that; that is, I went on making such far-fetched comparison. I have a book, Varinka, and there is the same thought in it, all very exactly described. I write this, my darling, because one has all sorts of dreams, you know. And now it's spring-time, so one's thoughts are always so pleasant; witty, amusing, and tender dreams visit one; everything is in a rosy light. That is why I have written all this; though, indeed, I took it all out of the book. The author there expresses the same desire in verse and writes:

"Why am I not a bird, a bird of prey!"

And so on, and so on. There are all sorts of thoughts in it, but never mind them now!

Oh, where were you going this morning, Varvara Alexyevna? Before I had begun to get ready for the office, you flew out of your room exactly like a bird of the air and crossed the yard, looking so gay. How glad it made me to look at you! Ah, Varinka, Varinka!—You must not be sad; tears are no help to sorrow; I know that, my dear, I know it from experience. Now you are so comfortable and you are getting a little stronger, too.

Well, how is your Fedora? Ah, what a good-natured woman she is! You must write and tell me, Varinka, how you get on with her now and whether you are satisfied with everything. Fedora is rather a grumbler; but you must not mind that, Varinka. God bless her! She has such a good heart. I have written to you already about Teresa here—she, too, is a good-natured and trustworthy woman. And how uneasy I was about our letters! How were they to be delivered? And behold the Lord sent us Teresa to make us happy. She is a good-natured woman, mild and long-suffering. But our landlady is simply merciless. She squeezes her at work like a rag.

Well, what a hole I have got into, Varvara Alexyevna! It is a lodging! I used to live like a bird in the woods, as you know yourself—it was so quiet and still that if a fly flew across the room you could hear it. Here it is all noise, shouting, uproar! But of course you don't know how it is all arranged here. Imagine a long passage, absolutely dark and very dirty. On the right hand there is a blank wall, and on the left, doors and doors, like the rooms in a hotel, in a long row. Well, these are lodgings and there is one room in each; there are people living by twos and by threes in one room. It is no use expecting order—it is a regular Noah's ark! They seem good sort of people, though, all so well educated and learned. One is in the service, a well-read man (he is somewhere in the literary department): he talks about Homer and Brambeus and authors of all sorts: he talks about everything; a very intelligent man! There are two officers who do nothing but play cards. There is a naval man; and an English teacher.

Wait a bit, I will divert you, my darling; I will describe them satirically in my next letter; that is, I will tell you what they are like in full detail. Our landlady is a very untidy little old woman, she goes about all day long in slippers and a dressing-gown, and all day long she is scolding at Teresa. I live in the kitchen, or rather, to be more accurate, there is a room near the kitchen (and our kitchen, I ought to tell you, is clean, light and very nice), a little room, a modest corner . . . or rather the kitchen is a big room of three windows so I have a partition running along the inside wall, so that it makes as it were another room, an extra lodging; it is roomy and comfortable, and there is a window and all—in fact, every convenience. Well, so that is my little corner. So don't you imagine, my darling, there is anything else about it, any mysterious significance in it; "here he is living in the kitchen!" you'll say. Well, if you like, I really am living in the kitchen, behind the partition, but that is nothing; I am quite private, apart from everyone, quiet and snug. I have put in a bed, a table, a chest of drawers and a couple of chairs, and I have hung up the ikon. It is true there are better lodgings—perhaps there may be much better, but convenience is the great thing; I have arranged it all for my own convenience, you know, and you must not imagine it is for anything else. Your little window is opposite, across the yard; and the yard is narrow, one catches glimpses of you passing—it is more cheerful for a poor, lonely fellow like me, and cheaper, too. The very cheapest room here with board costs thirty-five roubles in paper: beyond my means; but my lodging costs me seven roubles in paper and my board five in silver—that is, twenty-four and a half, and before I used to pay thirty and make it up by going without a great many things. I did not always have tea, but now I can spare enough for tea and sugar, too. And you know, my dear, one is ashamed as it were not to drink tea; here they are all well-to-do people so one feels ashamed. One drinks it, Varinka, for the sake of the other people, for the look of the thing; for myself I don't care, I am not particular. Think, too, of pocket-money—one must have a certain amount—then some sort of boots and clothes—is there much left? My salary is all I have. I am content and don't repine. It is sufficient. It has been sufficient for several years; there are extras, too.

Well, good-bye, my angel. I have bought a couple of pots of balsam and geranium—quite cheap—but perhaps you love mignonette? Well, there is mignonette, too, you write and tell me; be sure to write me everything as fully as possible, you know. Don't you imagine anything, though, or have any doubts about my having taken such a room, Varinka dear; no, it is my own convenience made me take it, and only the convenience of it tempted me. I am putting by money, you know, my darling, I am saving up: I have quite a lot of money. You must not think I am such a softy that a fly might knock me down with his wing. No, indeed, my own, I am not a fool, and I have as strong a will as a man of resolute and tranquil soul ought to have. Good-bye, my angel! I have scribbled you almost two sheets and I ought to have been at the office long ago. I kiss your fingers, my own, and remain

Your humble and faithful friend
MAKAR DYEVUSHKIN.

P.S.—One thing I beg you: answer me as fully as possible, my angel. I am sending you a pound of sweets with this, Varinka. You eat them up and may they do you good, and for God's sake do not worry about me and make a fuss. Well, good-bye then, my precious.

April 8.

DEAR SIR, MAKAR ALEXYEVITCH,

Do you know I shall have to quarrel with you outright at last. I swear to you, dear Makar Alexyevitch, that it really hurts me to take your presents. I know what they cost you, how you deny yourself, and deprive yourself of what is necessary. How many times have I told you that I need nothing, absolutely nothing; that I shall never be able to repay you for the kindnesses you have showered upon me? And why have you sent me these flowers? Well, the balsams I don't mind, but why the geranium? I have only to drop an incautious word, for instance, about that geranium, and you rush off and buy it. I am sure it must have been expensive? How charming the flowers are! Crimson, in little crosses. Where did you get such a pretty geranium? I have put it in the middle of the window in the most conspicuous place; I am putting a bench on the floor and arranging the rest of the flowers on the bench; you just wait until I get rich myself! Fedora is overjoyed; it's like paradise now, in our room—so clean, so bright!

Now, why those sweets? Upon my word, I guessed at once from your letter that there was something amiss with you—nature and spring and the sweet scents and the birds chirping. "What's this," I thought, "isn't it poetry?" Yes, indeed, your letter ought to have been in verse, that was all that was wanting, Makar Alexyevitch! There are the tender sentiments and dreams in roseate hues—everything in it! As for the curtain, I never thought of it; I suppose it got hitched up of itself when I moved the flower-pots, so there!

Ah, Makar Alexyevitch! Whatever you may say, however you may reckon over your income to deceive me, to prove that your money is all spent on yourself, you won't take me in and you won't hide anything from me. It is clear that you are depriving yourself of necessities for my sake. What possessed you, for instance, to take such a lodging? Why, you will be disturbed and worried; you are cramped for room, uncomfortable. You love solitude, and here, goodness knows what you have all about you! You might live a great deal better, judging from your salary. Fedora says you used to live ever so much better than you do now. Can you have spent all your life like this in solitude, in privation, without pleasure, without a friendly affectionate word, a lodger among strangers? Ah, dear friend, how sorry I am for you! Take care of your health, anyway, Makar Alexyevitch! You say your eyes are weak; so you must not write by candlelight; why write? Your devotion to your work must be known to your superiors without that.

Once more I entreat you not to spend so much money on me. I know that you love me, but you are not well off yourself. . . . I got up this morning feeling gay, too. I was so happy; Fedora had been at work a long time and had got work for me, too. I was so delighted; I only went out to buy silk and then I set to work. The whole morning I felt so lighthearted, I was so gay! But now it is all black thoughts and sadness again; my heart keeps aching.

Ah, what will become of me, what will be my fate! What is painful is that I am in such uncertainty, that I have no future to look forward to, that I cannot even guess what will become of me. It is dreadful to look back, too. There is such sorrow in the past, and my heart is torn in two at the very memory of it. All my life I shall be in suffering, thanks to the wicked people who have ruined me.

It is getting dark. Time for work. I should have liked to have written to you of lots of things but I have not the time, I must get to work. I must make haste. Of course letters are a good thing; they make it more cheerful, anyway. But why do you never come to see us yourself? Why is that, Makar Alexyevitch? Now we are so near, you know, and sometimes you surely can make time. Please do come! I have seen your Teresa. She looks such a sickly creature; I felt sorry for her and gave her twenty kopecks. Yes! I was almost forgetting: you must write to me all about your life and your surroundings as fully as possible. What sort of people are they about you and do you get on with them? I am longing to know all that. Mind you write to me! To-day I will hitch up the curtain on purpose. You should go to bed earlier; last night I saw your light till midnight. Well, good-bye. To-day I am miserable and bored and sad! It seems it is an unlucky day! Good-bye.

> Yours,
> VARVARA DOBROSELOV.

April 8.

DEAR MADAM, VARVARA ALEXYEVNA,

Yes, dear friend, yes, my own, it seems it was a bad day for poor luckless me! Yes; you mocked at an old man like me, Varvara Alexyevna! It was my fault, though, entirely my fault! I ought not in my old age, with scarcely any hair on my head, to have launched out into lyrical nonsense and fine phrases. . . . And I will say more, my dear: man is sometimes a strange creature, very strange. My goodness! he begins talking of something and is carried away directly! And what comes of it, what does it lead to? Why, absolutely nothing comes of it, and it leads to such nonsense that—Lord preserve me! I am not angry, Varinka dear, only I am very much vexed to remember it all, vexed that I wrote to you in such a foolish, high-flown way. And I went to the office to-day so cock-a-hoop; there was such radiance in my heart. For no rhyme or reason there was a regular holiday in my soul; I felt so gay. I took up my papers eagerly—but what did it all amount to! As soon as I looked about me, everything was as before, grey and dingy. Still the same ink-spots, the same tables and papers, and I, too, was just the same; as I always have been, so I was still—so what reason was there to mount upon Pegasus? And what was it all due to? The sun peeping out and the sky growing blue! Was that it? And how could I talk of the scents of spring? when you never know what there may be in our yard under the windows! I suppose I fancied all that in my foolishness. You know a man does sometimes make such mistakes in his own feelings and writes nonsense. That is due to nothing but foolish, excessive warmth of heart.

I did not walk but crawled home. For no particular reason my head had begun to ache; well that, to be sure, was one thing on the top of another. (I suppose I got a chill to my spine.) I was so delighted with the spring, like a fool, that I went out in a thin greatcoat. And you were mistaken in my feelings, my dear!

You took my outpouring of them quite in the wrong way. I was inspired by fatherly affection—nothing but a pure fatherly affection, Varvara Alexyevna. For I take the place of a father to you, in your sad fatherless and motherless state; I say this from my soul, from a pure heart, as a relation. After all, though, I am but a distant relation, as the proverb says "only the seventh water on the jelly," still I am a relation and now your nearest relation and protector; seeing that where you had most right to look for protection and support you have met with insult and treachery. As for verses, let me tell you, my love, it would not be seemly for me in my old age to be making verses. Poetry is nonsense! Why, boys are thrashed at school nowadays for making poetry . . . so that is how it is, my dear. . . .

What are you writing to me, Varvara Alexyevna, about comfort, about quiet and all sorts of things? I am not particular, my dear soul, I am not exacting. I have never lived better than I am doing now; so why should I be hard to please in my old age? I am well fed and clothed and shod; and it is not for us to indulge our whims! We are not royalties! My father was not of noble rank and his income was less than mine for his whole family. I have not lived in the lap of luxury! However, if I must tell the truth, everything was a good deal better in my old lodging; it was more roomy and convenient, dear friend. Of course my present lodging is nice, even in some respects more cheerful, and more varied if you like; I have nothing to say against that but yet I regret the old one. We old, that is elderly people, get used to old things as though to something akin to us. The room was a little one, you know; the walls were . . . there, what is the use of talking! . . . the walls were like all other walls, they don't matter, and yet remembering all my past makes me depressed . . . it's a strange thing: it's painful, yet the memories are, as it were, pleasant. Even what was nasty, what I was vexed with at the time, is, as it were, purified from nastiness in my memory and presents itself in an attractive shape to my imagination. We lived peacefully, Varinka, I and my old landlady who is dead. I remember my old landlady with a sad feeling now. She was a good woman and did not charge me much for my lodging. She used to knit all sorts of rugs out of rags on needles a yard long. She used to do nothing else. We used to share light and fuel, so we worked at one table. She had a grand-daughter, Masha—I remember her quite a little thing. Now she must be a girl of thirteen. She was such a mischievous little thing—very merry, always kept us amused. And we lived together, the three of us. Sometimes in the long winter evenings we would sit down to the round table, drink a cup of tea and then set to work. And to keep Masha amused and out of mischief the old lady used to begin to tell tales. And what tales they were! A sensible intelligent man would listen to them with pleasure, let alone a child. Why, I used to light my pipe and be so interested that I forgot my work. And the child, our little mischief, would be so grave, she would lean her rosy cheek on her little hand, open her pretty little mouth and, if the story were the least bit terrible, she would huddle up to the old woman. And we liked to look at her; and did not notice how the candle wanted snuffing nor hear the wind roaring and the storm raging outside.

We had a happy life, Varinka, and we lived together for almost twenty years.

But how I have been prattling on! Perhaps you don't care for such a subject, and it is not very cheering for me to remember it, especially just now in the twilight. Teresa's busy about something, my head aches and my back aches a little, too. And my thoughts are so queer, they seem to be aching as well. I am sad to-day, Varinka!

What's this you write, my dear? How can I come and see you? My darling, what would people say? Why, I should have to cross the yard, our folks would notice it, would begin asking questions—there would be gossip, there would be scandal, they would put a wrong construction on it. No, my angel, I had better see you to-morrow at the evening service, that will be more sensible and more prudent for both of us. And don't be vexed with me, my precious, for writing you such a letter; reading it over I see it is all so incoherent. I am an old man, Varinka, and not well-educated; I had no education in my youth and now I could get nothing into my head if I began studying over again. I am aware, Varinka, that I am no hand at writing, and I know without anyone else pointing it out and laughing at me that if I were to try to write something more amusing I should only write nonsense.

I saw you at your window to-day, I saw you let down your blind. Good-bye, good-bye, God keep you! Good-bye, Varvara Alexyevna.

Your disinterested friend,
MAKAR DYEVUSHKIN.

P.S.—I can't write satirical accounts of anyone now, my dear. I am too old, Varvara Alexyevna, to be facetious, and I should make myself a laughing-stock; as the proverb has it: "those who live in glass houses should not throw stones."

April 9.

DEAR SIR, MAKAR ALEXYEVITCH,

Come, are not you ashamed, Makar Alexyevitch, my friend and benefactor, to be so depressed and naughty? Surely you are not offended! Oh, I am often too hasty, but I never thought that you would take my words for a biting jest. Believe me, I could never dare to jest at your age and your character. It has all happened through my thoughtlessness, or rather from my being horribly dull, and dullness may drive one to anything! I thought that you meant to make fun yourself in your letter. I felt dreadfully sad when I saw that you were displeased with me. No, my dear friend and benefactor, you are wrong if you ever suspect me of being unfriendly and ungrateful. In my heart I know how to appreciate all you have done for me, defending me from wicked people, from their persecution and hatred. I shall pray for you always, and if my prayer rises to God and heaven accepts it you will be happy.

I feel very unwell to-day. I am feverish and shivering by turns. Fedora is very anxious about me. There is no need for you to be ashamed to come and see us, Makar Alexyevitch; what business is it of other people's! We are acquaintances, and that is all about it. . . .

Good-bye, Makar Alexyevitch. I have nothing more to write now, and indeed I can't write; I am horribly unwell. I beg you once more not to be angry with me and to rest assured of the invariable respect and devotion,

With which I have the honour to remain,
Your most devoted and obedient servant,
VARVARA DOBROSELOV.

April 12.

DEAR MADAM, VARVARA ALEXYEVNA,

Oh, my honey, what is the matter with you! This is how you frighten me every time. I write to you in every letter to take care of yourself, to wrap yourself up, not to go out in bad weather, to be cautious in every way—and, my angel, you don't heed me. Ah, my darling, you are just like some child! Why, you are frail, frail as a little straw, I know that. If there is the least little wind, you fall ill. So you must be careful, look after yourself, avoid risks and not reduce your friends to grief and distress.

You express the desire, dear Varinka, to have a full account of my daily life and all my surroundings. I gladly hasten to carry out your wish, my dear. I will begin from the beginning, my love: it will be more orderly.

To begin with, the staircases to the front entrance are very passable in our house; especially the main staircase—it is clean, light, wide, all cast-iron and mahogany, but don't ask about the backstairs: winding like a screw, damp, dirty, with steps broken and the walls so greasy that your hand sticks when you lean against them. On every landing there are boxes, broken chairs and cupboards, rags hung out, windows broken, tubs stand about full of all sorts of dirt and litter, eggshells and the refuse of fish; there is a horrid smell . . . in fact it is not nice.

I have already described the arrangement of the rooms; it is convenient, there is no denying; that is true, but it is rather stuffy in them. I don't mean that there is a bad smell, but, if I may so express it, a rather decaying, acrid, sweetish smell. At first it makes an unfavourable impression, but that is of no consequence; one has only to be a couple of minutes among us and it passes off and you don't notice how it passes off for you begin to smell bad yourself, your clothes smell, your hands smell and everything smells—well, you get used to it. Siskins simply die with us. The naval man is just buying the fifth—they can't live in our air and that is the long and short of it. Our kitchen is big, roomy and light. In the mornings, it is true, it is rather stifling when they are cooking fish or meat and splashing and slopping water everywhere, but in the evening it is paradise. In our kitchen there is always old linen hanging on a line; and as my room is not far off, that is, is almost part of the kitchen, the smell of it does worry me a little; but no matter, in time one gets used to anything.

Very early in the morning the hubbub begins, people moving about, walking, knocking—everyone who has to is getting up, some to go to the office, others about their own business; they all begin drinking tea. The samovars for the most part belong to the landlady;

there are few of them, so we all use them in turn, and if anyone goes with his teapot out of his turn, he catch it.

I, for instance, the first time made that mistake, and . . . but why describe it? I made the acquaintance of everyone at once. The naval man was the first I got to know; he is such an open fellow, told me everything: about his father and mother, about his sister married to an assessor in Tula, and about the town of Kronstadt. He promised to protect me and at once invited me to tea with him. I found him in the room where they usually play cards. There they gave me tea and were very insistent that I should play a game of chance with them. Whether they were laughing at me or not I don't know, but they were losing the whole night and they were still playing when I went away. Chalk, cards—and the room so full of smoke that it made my eyes smart. I did not play and they at once observed that I was talking of philosophy. After that no one said another word to me the whole time; but to tell the truth I was glad of it. I am not going to see them now; it's gambling with them, pure gambling. The clerk in the literary department has little gatherings in the evening, too. Well, there it is nice, quiet, harmless and delicate; everything is on a refined footing.

Well, Varinka, I will remark in passing that our landlady is a very horrid woman and a regular old hag. You've seen Teresa. You know what she is like, as thin as a plucked, dried-up chicken. There are two of them in the house, Teresa and Faldoni. I don't know whether he has any other name, he always answers to that one and everyone calls him that. He is a red-haired, foul-tongued Finn, with only one eye and a snub nose: he is always swearing at Teresa, they almost fight.

On the whole life here is not exactly perfect at all times. . . .

If only all would go to sleep at once at night and be quiet—that never happens. They are for ever sitting somewhere playing, and sometimes things go on that one would be ashamed to describe. By now I have grown accustomed to it; but I wonder how people with families get along in such a Bedlam. There is a whole family of poor creatures living in one of our landlady's rooms, not in the same row with the other lodgings but on the other side, in a corner apart. They are quiet people! No one hears anything of them. They live in one little room dividing it with a screen. He is a clerk out of work, discharged from the service seven years ago for something. His name is Gorshkov—such a grey little man; he goes about in such greasy, such threadbare clothes that it is sad to see him; ever so much worse than mine. He is a pitiful, decrepit figure (we sometimes meet in the passage); his knees shake, his hands shake, his head shakes, from some illness I suppose, poor fellow. He is timid, afraid of everyone and sidles along edgeways; I am shy at times, but he is a great deal worse. His family consists of a wife and three children. The eldest, a boy, is just like his father, just as frail. The wife was once very good-looking, even now one can see it; she, poor thing, goes about in pitiful tatters. They are in debt to the landlady, I have heard, she is none too gracious to them. I have heard, too, that there is some unpleasant business hanging over Gorshkov in connection with which he lost his place. . . . Whether it is a lawsuit—whether he is to be tried, or prosecuted, or what, I can't tell you for certain. Poor they are, mercy on us! It is always still and quiet in their room as if no one were living there. There is no sound even of the children. And it never happens that the children frolic about and play, and that is a bad sign. One evening I happened to pass their door; it was unusually quiet in the house at the time; I heard a sobbing, then a whisper, then sobbing again as though they were crying but so quietly, so pitifully that it was heart-rending, and the thought of those poor creatures haunted me all night so that I could not get to sleep properly.

Well, good-bye, my precious little friend, Varinka. I have described everything to the best of my abilities. I have been thinking of nothing but you all day. My heart aches over you, my dear. I know, my love, you have no warm cloak. Ah! these Petersburg springs, these winds and rain mixed with snow—they'll be the death of me, Varinka! Such salubrious airs, Lord preserve us!

Don't scorn my description, my love. I have no style, Varinka, no style whatever. I only wish I had. I write just what comes into my head only to cheer you up with something. If only I had had some education it would have been a different matter, but how much education have I had? Not a ha'porth.

> Always your faithful friend,
> MAKAR DYEVUSHKIN.

April 25.

HONOURED SIR, MAKAR ALEXYEVITCH,

I met my cousin Sasha to-day! It is horrible! She will be ruined too, poor thing! I heard, too, from other sources that Anna Fyodorovna is still making inquiries about me. It seems as though she will never leave off persecuting me. She says that she wants to *forgive me,* to forget all the past and that she must come and see me. She says that you are no relation to me at all, that she is a nearer relation, that you have no right to meddle in our family affairs and that it is shameful and shocking to live on your charity and at your expense. . . . She says that I have

forgotten her hospitality, that she saved mother and me from starving
to death, perhaps, that she gave us food and drink, and for more than
a year and a half was put to expense on our account, and that besides
all that she forgave us a debt. Even mother she will not spare! and if
only poor mother knew how they have treated me! God sees it! . . .
Anna Fyodorovna says that I was so silly that I did not know how to
take advantage of my luck, that she put me in the way of good luck,
that she is not to blame for anything else, and that I myself was not
able or perhaps was not anxious to defend my own honour. Who was
to blame in that, great God! She says that Mr. Bykov was perfectly
right and that he would not marry just anybody who . . . but why
write it!

It is cruel to hear such falsehoods, Makar Alexyevitch! I can't tell
you what a state I am in now. I am trembling, crying, sobbing. I have
been two hours over writing this letter to you. I thought that at least
she recognised how wrongly she had treated me; and you see what she
is now!

For God's sake don't be alarmed, my friend, the one friend who
wishes me well! Fedora exaggerates everything, I am not ill. I only
caught cold a little yesterday when I went to the requiem service for
mother at Volkovo. Why did you not come with me? I begged you
so much to do so. Ah, my poor, poor mother, if she could rise from
the grave, if she could see how they have treated me!   V. D.

May 20.

MY DARLING VARINKA,

I send you a few grapes, my love; I am told they are good for a con-
valescent and the doctor recommends them for quenching the
thirst—simply for thirst. You were longing the other day for a few
roses, my darling, so I am sending you some now. Have you any
appetite, my love?—that is the most important thing.

Thank God, though, that it is all over and done with, and that our
troubles, too, will be soon at an end. We must give thanks to heaven!

As for books, I cannot get hold of them anywhere for the moment.
I am told there is a good book here written in very fine language; they
say it is good, I have not read it myself, but it is very much praised
here. I have asked for it and they have promised to lend it me, only
will you read it? You are so hard to please in that line; it is difficult to
satisfy your taste, I know that already, my darling. No doubt you want
poetry, inspiration, lyrics—well, I will get poems too, I will get anything; there is a manuscript book full of extracts here.

I am getting on very well. Please don't be uneasy about me, my dearie. What Fedora told you about me is all nonsense; you tell her that she told a lie, be sure to tell her so, the wicked gossip! . . . I have not sold my new uniform. And why should I . . . judge for yourself, why should I sell it? Here, I am told, I have forty roubles bonus coming to me, so why should I sell it? Don't you worry, my precious; she's suspicious, your Fedora, she's suspicious. We shall get on splendidly, my darling! Only you get well, my angel, for God's sake, get well. Don't grieve your old friend. Who told you I had grown thin? It is slander, slander again! I am well and hearty and getting so fat that I am quite ashamed. I am well fed and well content: the only thing is for you to get strong again!

    Come, good-bye, my angel; I kiss your little fingers,

And remain, always,

Your faithful friend,

MAKAR DYEVUSHKIN.

P.S.—Ah, my love, what do you mean by writing like that again? . . . What nonsense you talk! Why, how can I come and see you so often, my precious? I ask you how can I? Perhaps snatching a chance after dark; but there, there's scarcely any night at all now, at this season. As it was, my angel, I scarcely left you at all while you were ill, while you were unconscious; but really I don't know how I managed it all; and afterwards I gave up going to you for people had begun to be inquisitive and to ask questions. There had been gossip going about here, even apart from that. I rely upon Teresa; she is not one to talk; but think for yourself, my darling, what a to-do there will be when they find out everything about us. They will imagine something and what will they say then? So you must keep a brave heart, my darling, and wait until you are quite strong again; and then we will arrange a *rendezvous* somewhere out of doors.

June 1.

MY DEAR MAKAR ALEXYEVITCH,

    I so long to do something nice that will please you in return for all the care and trouble you have taken about me, and all your love for me, that at last I have overcome my disinclination to rummage in my chest and find my diary, which I am sending to you now. I began it in the happy time of my life. You used often to question me with curiosity about my manner of life in the past, my mother, Pokrovskoe, my time with Anna Fyodorovna and my troubles in the recent past, and you were so impatiently anxious to read the manuscript in which I took the fancy, God knows why, to record some moments of my life that I have no doubt the parcel I am sending will be a pleasure to you.

It made me sad to read it over. I feel that I am twice as old as when I wrote the last line in that diary. It was all written at different dates. Good-bye, Makar Alexyevitch! I feel horribly depressed now and often I am troubled with sleeplessness. Convalescence is a very dreary business!

V. D.

I

I was only fourteen when my father died. My childhood was the happiest time of my life. It began not here but far away in a province in the wilds. My father was the steward of Prince P.'s huge estate in the province of T——. We lived in one of the Prince's villages and led a quiet, obscure, happy life. . . . I was a playful little thing; I used to do nothing but run about the fields, the copses and the gardens, and no one troubled about me. My father was constantly busy about his work, my mother looked after the house; no one taught me anything, for which I was very glad. Sometimes at daybreak I would run away either to the pond or to the copse or to the hayfield or to the reapers—and it did not matter that the sun was baking, that I was running, I did not know where, away from the village, that I was scratched by the bushes, that I tore my dress. . . . I should be scolded afterwards at home, but I did not care for that.

And it seems to me that I should have been so happy if it had been my lot to have spent all my life in one place and never to have left the country. But I had to leave my native place while I was still a child. I was only twelve when we moved to Petersburg. Ah, how well I remember our sorrowful preparations! How I cried when I said good-bye to everything that was so dear to me. I remember that I threw myself on father's neck and besought him with tears to remain a little longer in the country. Father scolded me, mother wept; she said that we had to go, that we could not help it. Old Prince P—— was dead. His heirs had discharged father from his post. Father had some money in the hands of private persons in Petersburg. Hoping to improve his position he thought his presence here in person essential. All this I learnt from mother. We settled here on the Petersburg Side and lived in the same spot up to the time of father's death.

How hard it was for me to get used to our new life! We moved to Petersburg in the autumn. When we left the country it was a clear, warm, brilliant day; the work of the fields was over; huge stacks of wheat were piled up on the threshing-floors and flocks of birds were calling about the fields; everything was so bright and gay: here as we came into the town we found rain, damp autumn chilliness, muggy greyness, sleet and a crowd of new, unknown faces, unwelcoming, ill-humoured, angry! We settled in somehow. I remember we were all in such a fuss, so troubled and busy in arranging our new life. Father was never at home, mother had not a quiet minute—I was forgotten altogether. I felt sad getting up in the morning after the first night in our new abode—our windows looked out on a yellow fence. The street was always covered with mud. The passers-by were few and they were all muffled up, they were all so cold. And for whole days together it was terribly miserable and dreary at home. We had scarcely a relation or intimate acquaintance. Father was not on friendly terms with Anna Fyodorovna. (He was in her debt.) People came on business to us pretty often. Usually they quarrelled, shouted and made an uproar. After every visit father was ill-humoured and cross; he would walk up and down the room by the hour together, frowning and not saying a word to anyone. Mother was silent then and did not dare to speak to him. I used to sit in a corner over a book, still and quiet, not daring to stir.

Three months after we came to Petersburg I was sent to boarding-school. How sad I was at first with strangers! Everything was so cold, so unfriendly! The teachers had such loud voices, the girls laughed at me so and I was such a wild creature. It was so stern and exacting! The fixed hours for everything, the meals in common, the tedious teachers—all that at first fretted and harassed me. I could not even sleep there. I used to cry the whole night, the long, dreary, cold night. Sometimes when they were all repeating or learning their lessons in the evening I would sit over my French translation or vocabularies, not daring to move and dreaming all the while of our little home, of father, of mother, of our old nurse, of nurse's stories. . . . Oh, how I used to grieve! The most trifling thing in the house I would recall with pleasure. I would keep dreaming how nice it would be now at home! I should be sitting in our little room by the samovar with my own people; it would be so warm, so nice, so familiar. How, I used to think, I would hug mother now, how tightly, how warmly! One would think and think and begin crying softly from misery, choking back one's tears, and the vocabularies would never get into one's head. I could not learn my lessons for next day; all night I would dream of the teacher, the mistress, the girls; all night I would be repeating my lessons in my sleep and would not know them next day. They would make me kneel down and give me only one dish for dinner. I was so depressed and dejected. At first all the girls laughed at me and teased me and tried to confuse me when I was saying my lessons, pinched me when in rows we walked into dinner or tea, made complaints against me to the teacher for next to nothing. But how heavenly it was when nurse used to come for me on Saturday evening. I used to hug the old darling in a frenzy of joy. She would put on my things, and wrap me up, and could not keep pace with me, while I would chatter and chatter and tell her everything. I would arrive home gay and happy, would hug everyone as though I had been away for ten years. There would be explanations, talks; descriptions would begin. I would greet everyone, laugh, giggle, skip and run about. Then there would be serious conversations with father about our studies, our teachers, French, Lomond's grammar, and we were all so pleased and happy. It makes me happy even now to remember those minutes. I tried my very utmost to learn and please father. I saw he was spending his last farthing on me and God knows what straits he was in. Every day he grew more gloomy, more ill-humoured, more angry. His character was quite changed, his business was unsuccessful, he had a mass of debts. Mother was sometimes afraid to cry, afraid to say a word for fear of making father angry. She was getting quite ill, was getting thinner and thinner and had begun to have a bad cough.

When I came back from school I used to find such sad faces; mother weeping stealthily, father angry. Then there would be scolding and upbraiding. Father would begin saying that I was no joy, no comfort to them; that they were depriving themselves of everything for my sake and I could not speak French yet; in fact all his failures, all his misfortunes were vented on me and mother. And how could he worry poor mother! It was heartrending to look at her; her cheeks were hollow, her eyes were sunken, there was a hectic flush in her face.

I used to come in for more scolding than anyone. It always began with trifles, and goodness knows what it went on to. Often I did not understand what it was about. Everything was a subject of complaint! . . . French and my being a great dunce and that the mistress of our school was a careless, stupid woman; that she paid no attention to our morals, that father was still unable to find a job, that Lomond's was a very poor grammar and that Zapolsky's was very much better, that a lot of money had been thrown away on me, that I was an unfeeling, stony-hearted girl—in fact, though I, poor thing, was striving my utmost, repeating conversations and vocabularies, I was to blame for everything, I was responsible for everything! And this was not because father did not love me; he was devoted to mother and me, but it was just his character.

Anxieties, disappointments, failures worried my poor father to distraction; he became suspicious, bitter; often he was close upon despair, he began to neglect his health, caught cold and all at once fell ill. He did not suffer long, but died so suddenly, so unexpectedly that we were all beside ourselves with the shock for some days. Mother seemed stunned; I actually feared for her reason.

As soon as father was dead creditors seemed to spring up from everywhere and rushed upon us like a torrent. Everything we had we gave them. Our little house on Petersburg Side, which father had bought six months after moving to Petersburg, was sold too. I don't know how they settled the rest, but we were left without refuge, without sustenance. Mother was suffering from a wasting disease, we could not earn our bread, we had nothing to live on, ruin stared us in the face. I was then only just fourteen. It was at this point that Anna Fyodorovna visited us. She always said that she owned landed estates and that she was some sort of relation of ours. Mother said, too, that she was a relation, only a very distant one. While father was alive she never came to see us. She made her appearance now with tears in her eyes and said she felt great sympathy for us; she condoled with us on our loss and our poverty-stricken condition; added that it was father's own fault; that he had lived beyond his means, had borrowed right and left and that he had been too self-confident. She expressed a desire to be on more friendly terms with us, said we must let by-gones be by-gones; when mother declared she had never felt any hostility towards her, she shed tears, took mother to church and ordered a requiem service for the "dear man". (That was how she referred to father.) After that she was solemnly reconciled to mother.

After leading up to the subject in many lengthy preambles, Anna Fyodorovna first depicted in glaring colours our poverty-stricken and forlorn position, our helplessness and hopelessness, and then invited us, as she expressed it, to take refuge with her. Mother thanked her, but for a long time could not make up her mind to accept; but seeing that there was nothing else she could do and no help for it, she told Anna Fyodorovna at last that we would accept her offer with gratitude.

I remember as though it were to-day the morning on which we moved from Petersburg Side to Vassilyevsky Ostrov. It was a clear, dry, frosty autumn morning. Mother was crying. I felt horribly sad; my heart was torn and ached with a terrible inexplicable misery . . . it was a terrible time. . . .

II

At first till we—that is mother and I—had grown used to our new home we both felt strange and miserable at Anna Fyodorovna's. Anna Fyodorovna lived in a house of her own in Sixth Row. There were only five living-rooms in the house. In three of them lived Anna

Fyodorovna and my cousin Sasha, a child who was being brought up by her, an orphan, fatherless and motherless. Then we lived in one room, and in the last room, next to ours, there was a poor student called Pokrovsky who was lodging in the house.

Anna Fyodorovna lived very well, in a more wealthy style than one could have expected; but her fortune was mysterious and so were her pursuits. She was always in a bustle, was always full of business, she drove out and came back several times a day; but what she was doing, what she was in a fuss about and with what object she was busy I could never make out. She had a large and varied circle of acquaintances. Visitors were always calling upon her, and the queerest people, always on business of some sort and to see her for a minute. Mother always carried me off to my room as soon as the bell rang. Anna Fyodorovna was horribly vexed with mother for this and was continually repeating that we were too proud, that we were proud beyond our means, that we had nothing to be proud about, and she would go on like that for hours together. I did not understand these reproaches at the time and, in fact, it is only now that I have found out, or rather that I guess why mother could not make up her mind to live with Anna Fyodorovna. Anna Fyodorovna was a spiteful woman, she was continually tormenting us. To this day it is a mystery to me why it was she invited us to live with her. At first she was fairly nice to us, but afterwards she began to show her real character as soon as she saw we were utterly helpless and had nowhere else to go. Later on she became very affectionate to me, even rather coarsely affectionate and flattering, but at first I suffered in the same way as mother. Every minute she was upbraiding us, she did nothing but talk of her charitable deeds. She introduced us to outsiders as her poor relations—a helpless widow and orphan to whom in the kindness of her heart, out of Christian charity, she had given a home. At meals she watched every morsel we took, while if we did not eat, there would be a fuss again; she would say we were fastidious, that we should not be over-nice, that we should be thankful for what we had; that she doubted if we had had anything better in our own home. She was continually abusing father, saying that he wanted to be better than other people and much good that had done him; that he had left his wife and daughter penniless and that if they had not had a benevolent relation, a Christian soul with a feeling heart, then, God knows, they might have been rotting in the street and dying of hunger. What did she not say! It was not so much painful as disgusting to hear her.

Mother was continually crying; her health grew worse from day to day. She was visibly wasting, yet she and I worked from morning till night, taking in sewing, which Anna Fyodorovna very much disliked, she was continually saying that she was not going to have her house turned into a dress-maker's shop. But we had to have clothes; we had to lay by for unforeseen expenses; it was absolutely necessary to have money of our own. We saved on the off-chance, hoping we might be able in time to move elsewhere. But mother lost what little health was left her over work; she grew weaker every day. The disease sucked the life out of her like a worm and hurried her to the grave. I saw it all, I felt it all, I realised it all and suffered; it all went on before my eyes.

The days passed and each day was like the one before. We lived as quietly as if we were not in a town. Anna Fyodorovna calmed down by degrees as she began fully to recognise her power. Though, indeed, no one ever thought of contradicting her. We were separated from her rooms by the corridor, and Pokrovsky's room was, as I have mentioned before, next to ours. He used to teach Sasha French and German, history, geography—all the sciences, as Anna Fyodorovna said, and for this he had his board and lodging from her. Sasha was a very intelligent child, though playful and mischievous; she was thirteen. Anna Fyodorovna observed to mother that it would not be amiss if I were to have lessons, since my education had not been finished at the boarding-school, and for a whole year I shared Sasha's lessons with Pokrovsky. Pokrovsky was poor, very poor. His health had prevented him from continuing his studies and it was only from habit that he was called a student. He was so retiring, so quiet and so still that we heard no sound of him from our room. He was very queer-looking; he walked so awkwardly, bowed so awkwardly and spoke so queerly that at first I could not look at him without laughing. Sasha was continually mocking at him, especially when he was giving us our lessons. He was of an irritable temper, too, was constantly getting cross, was beside himself about every trifle, scolded us, complained of us, and often went off into his own room in anger without finishing the lesson. He used to sit for days together over his books. He had a great many books, and such rare and expensive books. He gave other lessons, too, for which he was paid, and as soon as ever he had money he would go and buy books.

In time I got to know him better and more intimately. He was a very kind and good young man, the best person it has been my lot to meet. Mother had a great respect for him. Afterwards he became the best of my friends—next to mother, of course.

At first, though I was such a big girl, I was as mischievous as Sasha. We used to rack our brains for hours together to find ways to tease him and exhaust his patience. His anger was extremely funny, and we used to find it awfully amusing. (I am ashamed even to think of it now.) Once we teased him almost to the point of tears and I distinctly heard him whisper, "Spiteful children." I was suddenly overcome with confusion; I felt ashamed and miserable and sorry for him. I remember that I blushed up to my ears and almost with tears in my eyes began begging him not to mind and not to be offended at our stupid mischief. But he closed the book and without finishing the lesson went off to his own room. I was torn with penitence all day long. The thought that we children had reduced him to tears by our cruelty was insufferable. So we had waited for his tears. So we had wanted them; so we had succeeded in driving him out of all patience; so we had forced him, a poor unfortunate man, to realise his hard lot.

I could not sleep all night for vexation, sorrow, repentance. They say repentance relieves the soul—on the contrary. There was an element of vanity mixed, I don't know how, with my sadness. I did not want him to look upon me as a child, I was fifteen then.

From that day I began worrying my imagination, creating thousands of plans to make Pokrovsky change his opinion about me. But I had become all of a sudden timid and shy; in my real position I could venture upon nothing and confined myself to dreams (and God knows what dreams!). I left off joining in Sasha's pranks; he left off being angry with us; but for my vanity that was little comfort.

Now I will say a few words about the strangest, most curious and most pathetic figure I have ever chanced to meet. I speak of him now, at this passage in my diary, because until that period I had hardly paid any attention to him. But now everything that concerned Pokrovsky had suddenly become interesting to me.

There used sometimes to come to the house a little old man, grey-headed, grubby, badly-dressed, clumsy, awkward, incredibly queer in fact. At the first glance at him one might imagine that he was, as it were, abashed by something—as it were, ashamed of himself. That is why he always seemed to be shrinking into himself, to be, as it were, cowering; he had such queer tricks and ways that one might almost have concluded he was not in his right mind. He would come to the house and stand at the glass door in the entry without daring to come in. If one of us passed by—Sasha or I or any one of the servants he knew to be rather kind to him—he would begin waving at once, beckoning, making gesticulations, and only when one nodded and called to him—a sign agreed upon that there was no outsider in the house and that he might come in when he liked—only then the old man stealthily opened the door with a smile of glee, and rubbing his hands with satisfaction, walked on tiptoe straight to Pokrovsky's room. This was Pokrovsky's father.

Later on, I learnt the whole story of this poor old man. He had once been in the service, was entirely without ability, and filled the very lowest and most insignificant post. When his first wife (our

Pokrovsky's mother) died he took it into his head to marry a second time and married a girl of the working-class. Everything was turned topsy-turvy under the rule of his new wife. She let no one live in peace, she domineered over everyone. Our Pokrovsky was still a child, ten years old. His stepmother hated him, but fate was kind to the boy. A country gentleman called Bykov, who had known the elder Pokrovsky and at one time been his patron, took the child under his protection and sent him to school. He was interested in him because he had known his mother, who had been a protégée of Anna Fyodorovna's and had by her been married to Pokrovsky. Mr. Bykov, a very intimate friend of Anna Fyodorovna's, had generously given the girl a dowry of five thousand roubles on her marriage. Where that money went to I don't know.

That was the story Anna Fyodorovna told me; young Pokrovsky never liked speaking of his family circumstances. They say his mother was very pretty, and it seems strange to me that she should have been so unfortunately married to such an insignificant man. He was quite young when she died four years after their marriage.

From boarding-school young Pokrovsky went on to a high school and then to the university. Mr. Bykov, who very often came to Petersburg, did not confine his protection to that. Owing to the breakdown of his health Pokrovsky could not continue his studies at the university. Mr. Bykov introduced him to Anna Fyodorovna, commended him to her good offices and so young Pokrovsky was taken into the house and was given his board on condition of teaching Sasha everything that was necessary. Old Pokrovsky was driven by grief at his wife's cruelty to the worst of vices and was scarcely ever sober. His wife used to beat him, make him live in the kitchen, and brought things at last to such a pass that he was quite accustomed to being beaten and ill-treated and did not complain of it. He was not a very old man, but his mind had almost given way owing to his bad habits. The one sign he showed of generous and humane feeling was his boundless love for his son. It was said that young Pokrovsky was as like his dead mother as one drop of water is like another. Maybe it was the memory of his first good wife that stirred in the ruined old man's heart this infinite love for his son. The old man could speak of nothing but his son and always visited him twice a week. He did not dare to come oftener, for young Pokrovsky could not endure his father's visits. Of all his failings, undoubtedly the greatest and foremost was his disrespect to his father. The old man certainly was at times the most insufferable creature in the world. In the first place he was horribly inquisitive, secondly, by remarks and questions of the most trivial and senseless kind he interrupted his son's work every minute, and, lastly, he would sometimes come under the influence of drink. The son gradually trained the old man to overcome his vices, his curiosity and incessant chatter, and at last had brought things to such a point that the old man obeyed him in everything like an oracle and did not dare open his mouth without permission.

The poor old man could not sufficiently admire and marvel at his Petinka (as he called his son). When he came to see him he almost always had a timid, careworn air, most likely from uncertainty as to the reception his son would give him. He was usually a long time making up his mind to come in, and if I happened to be there he would spend twenty minutes questioning me: "How was Petinka? Was he quite well? What sort of mood was he in, and was he busy over anything important? What was he doing? Was he writing, or absorbed in reflection?" When I had sufficiently cheered and reassured him, the old man at last ventured to come in, and very, very quietly, very, very cautiously opened the door, first poked in his head, and if his son nodded to him and the old man saw he was not angry, he moved stealthily into the room, took off his overcoat and his hat, which was always crushed, full of holes and with a broken brim, hung them on a hook, did everything quietly, noiselessly; then cautiously sat down on a chair, never taking his eyes off his son, watching every movement and trying to guess what mood his "Petinka" was in. If his son seemed ever so little out of humour and the old man noticed it, he got up from his seat at once and explained, "I just looked in, Petinka, only for a minute. I have been out for a long walk, I was passing and came in for a rest." And then, dumbly, submissively he would take his coat, his wretched hat, again he would stealthily open the door and go away, keeping a forced smile on his face to check the rush of disappointment in his heart and to hide it from his son.

But when the son made the father welcome, the old man was beside himself with joy. His face, his gestures, his movements all betrayed his pleasure. If his son began talking to him, the old man always rose a little from the chair and answered softly, deferentially, almost with reverence, always trying to use the choicest, that is, the most absurd expressions. But he was not blessed with the gift of words; he was always nervous and confused, so that he did not know what to do with his hands, what to do with himself, and kept whispering the answer to himself long afterwards as though trying to correct himself. If he did succeed in giving a good answer, the old man smoothed himself down, straightened his waistcoat, his tie, his coat and assumed an air of dignity. Sometimes he plucked up so much courage and grew so bold that he stealthily got up from his chair, went up to the bookshelf, took down some book and even began reading something on the spot, whatever the book might be. All this he did with an air of assumed unconcern and coolness, as though he could always do what he liked with his son's books, as though his son's graciousness was nothing out of the way.

But I once happened to see how frightened the poor fellow was when Pokrovsky asked him not to touch the books. He grew nervous and confused, put the book back upside down, then tried to right it, turned it round and put it in with the edges outside; smiled, flushed and did not know how to efface his crime. Pokrovsky by his persuasions did succeed in turning the old man a little from his evil propensities, and whenever the son saw his father sober three times running he would give him twenty-five kopecks, fifty kopecks, or more at parting. Sometimes he would buy his father a pair of boots, a tie or a waistcoat; then the old man was as proud as a cock in his new clothes.

Sometimes he used to come to us. He used to bring Sasha and me gingerbread cocks and apples and always talked to us of Petinka. He used to beg us to be attentive and obedient at lessons, used to tell us that Petinka was a good son, an exemplary son and, what was more, a learned son. Meanwhile he would wink at us so funnily with his left eye and make such amusing grimaces that we could not help smiling, and went into peals of laughter at him. Mother was very fond of him. But the old man hated Anna Fyodorovna, though he was stiller than water, humbler than grass in her presence.

Soon I left off having lessons with Pokrovsky. As before, he looked upon me as a child, a mischievous little girl on a level with Sasha. This hurt me very much, for I was trying my utmost to efface the impression of my behaviour in the past, but I was not noticed. That irritated me more and more. I scarcely ever spoke to Pokrovsky except at our lessons, and indeed I could not speak. I blushed and was confused, and afterwards shed tears of vexation in some corner.

I do not know how all this would have ended if a strange circumstance had not helped to bring us together. One evening when mother was sitting with Anna Fyodorovna I went stealthily into Pokrovsky's room. I knew he was not at home, and I really don't know what put it into my head to go into his room. Until that moment I had never peeped into it, though we had lived next door for over a year. This time my heart throbbed violently, so violently that it seemed it would leap out of my bosom. I looked around with peculiar curiosity. Pokrovsky's room was very poorly furnished: it was untidy. Papers were lying on the table and the chairs. Books and papers! A strange thought came to me, and at the same time an unpleasant feeling of vexation took possession of me. It seemed to me that my affection, my loving heart were little to him. He was learned while I was stupid, and knew nothing, had read nothing, not a single book . . . at that point I looked enviously at the long shelves which were almost breaking down under the weight of the books. I was overcome by anger, misery, a sort of fury. I longed and at once determined to read his books, every one of them, and as quickly as possible. I don't know, perhaps I thought that when I learned all he knew I should be more worthy of his friendship. I rushed to the first shelf; without stopping to think I seized the first dusty old volume; flushing and turning pale by turns, trembling with excitement and dread, I carried off the stolen book, resolved to read it at night—by the nightlight while mother was asleep.

But what was my vexation when, returning to our room, I hurriedly opened the book and saw it was some old work in Latin. It was half decayed and worm-eaten. I went back without loss of time. Just as I was trying to put the book back in the shelf I heard a noise in the passage and approaching footsteps. I tried with nervous haste to be quick, but the insufferable book had been so tightly wedged in the shelf that when I took it out all the others had shifted and packed closer of themselves, so now there was no room for their former companion. I had not the strength to force the book in. I pushed the books with all my might, however. The rusty nail which supported the shelf, and which seemed to be waiting for that moment to break, broke. One end of the shelf fell down. The books dropped noisily on the floor in all directions. The door opened and Pokrovsky walked into the room.

I must observe that he could not bear anyone to meddle in his domain. Woe to anyone who touched his books! Imagine my horror when the books, little and big, of all sizes and shapes dashed off the shelf, flew dancing under the table, under the chairs, all over the room! I would have run, but it was too late. It is all over, I thought, it is all over. I am lost, I am done for! I am naughty and mischievous like a child of ten, I am a silly chit of a girl! I am a great fool!

Pokrovsky was dreadfully angry.

"Well, this is the last straw!" he shouted. "Are not you ashamed to be so mischievous? . . . Will you ever learn sense?" and he rushed to collect his books. "Don't, don't!" he shouted. "You would do better not to come where you are not invited."

A little softened, however, by my humble movement, he went on more quietly, in his usual lecturing tone, speaking as though he were still my teacher:

"Why, when will you learn to behave properly and begin to be sensible? You should look at yourself. You are not a little child. You are not a little girl. Why, you are fifteen!"

And at that point, probably to satisfy himself that I was not a little girl, he glanced at me and blushed up to his ears. I did not understand. I stood before him staring in amazement. He got up, came towards me with an embarrassed air, was horribly confused, said something, seemed to be apologising for something, perhaps for having only just noticed that I was such a big girl. At last I understood. I don't remember what happened to me then; I was overcome with confusion, lost my head, blushed even more crimson than Pokrovsky, hid my face in my hands and ran out of the room.

I did not know what to do, where to hide myself for shame. The mere fact that he had found me in his room was enough! For three whole days I could not look at him: I blushed until the tears came into my eyes. The most absurd ideas whirled through my brain. One of them—the maddest—was a plan to go to him, explain myself to him, confess everything to him, tell him all openly and assure him I had not behaved like a silly little girl but had acted with good intentions. I quite resolved to go but, thank God, my courage failed me. I can imagine what a mess I should have made of it! Even now I am ashamed to remember it all.

A few days later mother suddenly became dangerously ill. After two days in bed, on the third night, she was feverish and delirious. I did not sleep all one night, looking after mother, sitting by her bedside, bringing her drink and giving her medicine at certain hours. The second night I was utterly exhausted. At times I was overcome with sleep, my head went round and everything was green before my eyes. I was ready any minute to drop with fatigue, but mother's weak moans roused me, I started up, waked for an instant and then was overwhelmed with drowsiness again. I was in torment. I don't know, I cannot remember, but some horrible dream, some awful apparition haunted my over-wrought brain at the agonising moment of struggling between sleeping and waking. I woke up in terror. The room was dark; the night-light had burned out. Streaks of light suddenly filled the whole room, gleamed over the wall and disappeared. I was frightened, a sort of panic came over me. My imagination had been upset by a horrible dream, my heart was oppressed with misery. . . . I leapt up from my chair and unconsciously shrieked from an agonising, horribly oppressive feeling. At that moment the door opened and Pokrovsky walked into our room.

All I remember is that I came to myself in his arms. He carefully put me in a low chair, gave me a glass of water and showered questions on me. I don't remember what I answered.

"You are ill, you are very ill yourself," he said, taking my hand. "You are feverish, you will kill yourself. You do not think of your health; calm yourself, lie down, go to sleep. I will wake you in two hours time. Rest a little . . . lie down, lie down!" not letting me utter a word in objection. I was too tired to object; my eyes were closing with weakness. I lay down in a low chair, resolved to sleep only half an hour, and slept till morning. Pokrovsky only waked me when the time came to give mother her medicine.

The next evening when, after a brief rest in the daytime, I made ready to sit up by mother's bedside again, firmly resolved not to fall asleep this time, Pokrovsky at eleven o'clock knocked at the door. I opened it.

"It is dull for you, sitting alone," he said to me. "Here is a book; take it, it won't be so dull, anyway."

I took it; I don't remember what the book was like; I hardly glanced into it, though I did not sleep all night. A strange inward excitement would not let me sleep; I could not remain sitting still; several times I got up from the chair and walked about the room. A sort of inward content was suffused through my whole being. I was so glad of Pokrovsky's attention. I was proud of his anxiety and uneasiness about me. I spent the whole night, musing and dreaming. Prokrovsky did not come in again, and I knew he would not come, and I wondered about the following evening.

The next evening, when everyone in the house had gone to bed, Pokrovsky opened his door and began talking to me, standing in the doorway of his room. I do not remember now a single word of what we said to one another; I only remember that I was shy, confused, vexed with myself and looked forward impatiently to the end of the conversation, though I had been desiring it intensely, dreaming of it all day, and making up my questions and answers. . . . The first stage of our friendship began from that evening. All through mother's illness we spent several hours together every night. I got over my shyness by degrees, though after every conversation I found something in it to be vexed with myself about. Yet with secret joy and proud satisfaction I saw that for my sake he was beginning to forget his insufferable books.

By chance the conversation once turned in jest on his books having fallen off the shelf. It was a strange moment. I was, as it were, *too* open and candid. I was carried away by excitement and a strange enthusiasm, and I confessed everything to him. . . . Confessed that I longed to study, to know something, that it vexed me to be considered a little girl. . . . I repeat that I was in a very strange mood; my heart was soft, there were tears in my eyes—I concealed nothing and told him everything—everything—my affection for him, my desire to love him, to live with him, to comfort him, to console him. He looked

at me somewhat strangely, with hesitation and perplexity, and did not
say one word. I felt all at once horribly sore and miserable. It seemed
to me that he did not understand me, that perhaps he was laughing at
me. I suddenly burst out crying like a child, I could not restrain
myself, and sobbed as though I were in a sort of fit. He took my hands,
kissed them and pressed them to his heart; talked to me, comforted
me; he was much touched. I do not remember what he said to me,
only I kept on crying and laughing and crying again, blushing, and so
joyful that I could not utter a word. In spite of my emotion, I noticed,
however, that Pokrovsky still showed traces of embarrassment and
constraint. It seemed as though he were overwhelmed with wonder at
my enthusiasm, my delight, my sudden warm, ardent affection.
Perhaps it only seemed strange to him at first; later on his hesitation
vanished and he accepted my devotion to him, my friendly words, my
attentions, with the same simple, direct feeling that I showed, and
responded to it all with the same attentiveness, as affectionately and
warmly as a sincere friend, a true brother. My heart felt so warm, so
happy. . . . I was not reserved, I concealed nothing from him, he saw it
all and grew every day more and more attached to me.

And really I do not remember what we used to talk about in those
tormenting, and at the same time happy, hours when we met at night
by the flickering light of a little lamp, and almost by my poor mother's
bedside. . . . We talked of everything that came into our minds, that
broke from our hearts, that craved expression, and we were almost
happy. . . . Oh, it was a sad and joyful time, both at once. . . . And it
makes me both sad and joyful now to think of him. Memories are
always tormenting, whether they are glad or bitter; it is so with me,
anyway; but even the torment is sweet. And when the heart grows
heavy, sick, weary and sad, then memories refresh and revive it, as the
drops of dew on a moist evening after a hot day refresh and revive a
poor sickly flower, parched by the midday heat.

Mother began to get better, but I still sat up by her bedside at night.
Pokrovsky used to give me books; at first I read them to keep myself
awake; then more attentively, and afterwards with eagerness. They
opened all at once before me much that was new, unknown and unfa-
miliar. New thoughts, new impressions rushed in a perfect flood into
my heart. And the more emotion, the more perplexity and effort it
cost me to assimilate those new impressions, the dearer they were to
me and the more sweetly they thrilled my soul. They crowded upon
my heart all at once, giving it no rest. A strange chaos began to trouble my whole being. But that spiritual commotion could not upset my
balance altogether. I was too dreamy and that saved me.

When mother's illness was over, our long talks and evening interviews were at an end; we succeeded sometimes in exchanging words, often trivial and of little consequence, but I was fond of giving everything its significance, its peculiar underlying value. My life was full, I was happy, calmly, quietly happy. So passed several weeks. . . .

One day old Pokrovsky came to see us. He talked to us for a long time, was exceptionally gay, cheerful and communicative, he laughed, made jokes after his fashion, and at last explained the mystery of his ecstatic condition, and told us that that day week would be Petinka's birthday and that for the occasion he should come and see his son; that he should put on a new waistcoat and that his wife had promised to buy him new boots. In fact, the old man was completely happy and chatted away of everything in his mind. His birthday! That birthday gave me no rest day or night. I made up my mind to give Pokrovsky something as a sign of my affection. But what? At last I thought of giving him books. I knew he wanted to have Pushkin's works in the latest, complete edition, and I decided to buy Pushkin. I had thirty roubles of my own money earned by needlework. The money had been saved up to buy me a dress. I promptly sent old Matrona, our cook, to find out what the whole of Pushkin cost. Alas! The price of the eleven volumes, including the cost of binding, was at least sixty roubles. Where could I get the money? I thought and thought and did not know what to decide upon. I did not want to ask mother. Of course mother would have certainly helped me; but then everyone in the house would have known of our present; besides, the present would have become a token of gratitude in repayment for all that Pokrovsky had done for us during the past year. I wanted to give it alone and no one else to know of it. And for what he had done for me I wanted to be indebted to him for ever without any sort of repayment except my affection.

At last I found a way out of my difficulty.

I knew at the second-hand shops in the Gostiny Dvor one could sometimes, with a little bargaining, buy at half-price a book hardly the worse for wear and almost completely new. I resolved to visit the Gostiny Dvor. As it happened, next day some things had to be bought for us and also for Anna Fyodorovna. Mother was not very well, and Anna Fyodorovna, very luckily, was lazy, so that it fell to me to make these purchases and I set off with Matrona.

I was so fortunate as to find a Pushkin very quickly and one in a very fine binding. I began bargaining. At first they demanded a price higher than that in the bookseller's shops; but in the end, though not without trouble, and walking away several times, I brought the shopman to knocking down the price and asking no more than ten roubles in silver. How I enjoyed bargaining! . . . Poor Matrona could not make out what was the matter with me and what possessed me to buy so many books. But, oh, horror! My whole capital consisted of thirty roubles in paper, and the shopman would not consent to let the books go cheaper. At last I began beseeching him, begged and begged him and at last persuaded him. He gave way but only took off two and a half roubles and swore he only made that concession for my sake because I was such a nice young lady and he would not have done it for anyone else. I still had not enough by two and a half roubles. I was ready to cry with vexation. But the most unexpected circumstance came to my assistance in my distress.

Not far off at another bookstall I saw old Pokrovsky. Four or five second-hand dealers were clustering about him; they were bewildering him completely and he was at his wits' end. Each of them was profering his wares and there was no end to the books they offered and he longed to buy. The poor old man stood in the midst of them, looking a disconsolate figure and did not know what to choose from what was offered him. I went up and asked him what he was doing here. The old man was delighted to see me; he was extremely fond of me, hardly less than of his Petinka, perhaps.

"Why, I'm buying books, Varvara Alexyevna," he answered. "I am buying books for Petinka. Here it will soon be his birthday and he is fond of books, so, you see, I am going to buy them for him. . . ."

The old man always expressed himself in a very funny way and now he was in the utmost confusion besides. Whatever he asked the price of, it was always a silver rouble, or two or three silver roubles; he had by now given up inquiring about the bigger books and only looked covetously at them, turning over the leaves, weighing them in his hands and putting them back again in their places.

"No, no, that's dear," he would say in an undertone, "but maybe there'll be something here."

And then he would begin turning over thin pamphlets, songbooks, almanacs; these were all very cheap.

"But why do you want to buy those?" I asked him. "They are all awful rubbish."

"Oh, no," he answered. "No, you only look what good little books there are here. They are very, very good little books!"

And the last words he brought out in such a plaintive sing-song that I fancied he was ready to cry with vexation at the good books being so dear, and in another moment a tear would drop from his pale cheeks on his red nose. I asked him whether he had plenty of money.

"Why, here," the poor fellow pulled out at once all his money wrapped up in a piece of greasy newspaper. "Here there's half a rouble, a twenty-kopeck piece and twenty kopecks in copper."

I carried him off at once to my second-hand bookseller.

"Here, these eleven volumes cost only thirty-two roubles and a half; I have thirty; put your two and a half to it and we will buy all these books and give them to him together."

The old man was beside himself with delight, he shook out all his money, and the bookseller piled all our purchased volumes upon him. The old man stuffed volumes in all his pockets, carried them in both hands and under his arms and bore them all off to his home, giving me his word to bring them all to me in secret next day.

Next day the old man came to see his son, spent about an hour with him as usual, then came in to us and sat down beside me with a very comical mysterious air. Rubbing his hands in proud delight at being in possession of a secret, he began with a smile by telling me that all the books had been conveyed here unnoticed and were standing in a corner in the kitchen under Matrona's protection. Then the conversation naturally passed to the day we were looking forward to; the old man talked at length of how we would give our present, and the more absorbed he became in the subject the more apparent it was to me that he had something in his heart of which he could not, dared not, speak, which, in fact, he was afraid to put into words. I waited and said nothing. The secret joy, the secret satisfaction which I had readily discerned at first in his strange gestures and grimaces and the winking of his left eye, disappeared. Every moment he grew more uneasy and disconsolate; at last he could not contain himself.

"Listen," he began timidly in an undertone.

"Listen, Varvara Alexyevna . . . do you know what, Varvara Alexyevna . . . ?" The old man was in terrible confusion. "When the day of his birthday comes, you know, you take ten books and give them yourself, that is from yourself, on your own account; I'll take only the eleventh, and I, too, will give it from myself, that is, apart, on my own account. So then, do you see—you will have something to give, and I shall have something to give; we shall both have something to give."

At this point the old man was overcome with confusion and relapsed into silence. I glanced at him; he was waiting for my verdict with timid expectation.

"But why do you want us not to give them together, Zahar Petrovitch?"

"Why, you see, Varvara Alexyevna, it's just . . . it's only, you know . . ."

In short, the old man faltered, flushed, got stuck in his sentence and could not proceed.

"You see," he explained at last, "Varvara Alexyevna, I indulge at times . . . that is, I want to tell you that I am almost always indulging, constantly indulging . . . I have a habit which is very bad . . . that is, you know, it's apt to be so cold outdoors and at times there are unpleasantnesses of all sorts, or something makes one sad, or something happens amiss and then I give way at once and begin to indulge and sometimes drink too much. Petrushka dislikes that very much. He gets angry with me, do you see, Varvara Alexyevna, scolds me and gives me lectures, so that I should have liked now to show him by my present that I am reforming and beginning to behave properly, that here I've saved up to buy the book, saved up for ever so long, for I scarcely ever have any money except it may happen Petrushka gives me something. He knows that. So here he will see how I have used my money and will know that I have done all that only for him.

I felt dreadfully sorry for the old man. I thought for a moment. The old man looked at me uneasily.

"Listen, Zahar Petrovitch," I said; "you give him them all."

"How all? Do you mean all the books?"

"Why, yes, all the books."

"And from myself?"

"Yes, from yourself."

"From myself alone? Do you mean on my own account?"

"Why yes, on your own account."

I believe I made my meaning very clear, but it was a long time before the old man could understand me.

"Why yes," he said, after pondering. "Yes! That would be very nice, but how about you, Varvara Alexyevna?"

"Oh, well, I shall give nothing."

"What!" cried the old man, almost alarmed. "So you don't want to give Petinka anything?"

The old man was dismayed; at that moment he was ready, I believe, to give up his project in order that I might be able to give his son something. He was a kind-hearted old fellow! I assured him that I should have been glad to give something, but did not want to deprive him of the pleasure.

"If your son is satisfied and you are glad," I added, "then I shall be glad, for I shall feel secretly in my heart as though I were really giving it myself."

With that the old man was completely satisfied. He spent another two hours with us, but could not sit still in his place and was continually getting up, fussing noisily about, playing with Sasha, stealthily kissing me, pinching my hand and making faces at Anna Fyodorovna on the sly. Anna Fyodorovna turned him out of the house at last. The old man was, in fact, in his delight, more excited than he had perhaps ever been before.

On the festive day he appeared exactly at eleven o'clock, coming straight from mass in a decently mended swallow-tail coat and actually wearing a new waistcoat and new boots. He had a bundle of books in each hand. We were all sitting drinking coffee in Anna Fyodorovna's drawing-room at the time (it was Sunday). The old man began by saying, I believe, that Pushkin was a very fine poet; then, with much hesitation and confusion, he passed suddenly to the necessity of one's behaving oneself properly, and that if a man does not behave properly then he will indulge; that bad habits are the ruin and destruction of a man; he even enumerated several fatal instances of intemperance, and wound up by saying that for some time past he had been completely reformed and his behaviour now was excellent and exemplary; that he had even, in the past, felt the justice of his son's exhortations, that he felt it all long ago and laid it to heart, but now he had begun to control himself in practice, too. In proof of which he presented himself with the books bought with money which he had saved up during a long period of time.

I could not help laughing and crying as I listened to the poor old man; so he knew how to lie on occasion! The books were carried into Pokrovsky's room and arranged on the shelves. Pokrovsky at once guessed the truth. The old man was invited to dinner. We were all so merry that day; after dinner we played forfeits and cards; Sasha was in wild spirits and I was hardly less so. Pokrovsky was attentive to me and kept seeking an opportunity to speak to me alone, but I would not let him. It was the happiest day of all those four years of my life.

And now come sad, bitter memories, and I begin the story of my gloomy days. That is why, perhaps, my pen moves more slowly and seems to refuse to write more. That is why, perhaps, I have dwelt in memory with such eagerness and such love on the smallest details of my trivial existence in my happy days. Those days were so brief; they were followed by grief, black grief, and God only knows when it will end.

My troubles began with the illness and death of Pokrovsky.

He fell ill about two months after the last incidents I have described here. He spent those two months in unceasing efforts to secure some means of subsistence, for he still had no settled position. Like all consumptives he clung up to the very last moment to the hope of a very long life. A post as a teacher turned up for him, but he had a great distaste for that calling. He could not take a place in a government office on account of his health. Besides, he would have had to wait a long time for the first instalment of his salary. In short, Pokrovsky met with nothing but disappointment on all sides and this tried his temper. His health was suffering, but he paid no attention to it. Autumn was coming on, every day he went out in his thin little overcoat to try and get work, to beg and implore for a place, which was inwardly an agony to him; he used to get his feet wet and to be soaked through with the rain, and at last he took to his bed and never got up from it again. . . . He died in the middle of autumn at the end of October.

I scarcely left his room during the whole time of his illness, I nursed him and looked after him. Often I did not sleep for nights together. He was frequently delirious and rarely quite himself; he talked of goodness knows what, of his post, of his books, of me, of his father . . . and it was then I heard a great deal about his circumstances of which I had not known or even guessed before. When first he was ill, all of them looked at me somehow strangely; Anna Fyodorovna shook her head. But I looked them all straight in the face and they did not blame me any more for my sympathy for Pokrovsky—at least my mother did not.

Sometimes Pokrovsky knew me, but this was seldom. He was almost all the time unconscious. Sometimes for whole nights together he would carry on long, long conversations with someone in obscure, indistinct words and his hoarse voice resounded with a hollow echo in his narrow room as in a coffin; I used to feel terrified then. Especially on the last night he seemed in a frenzy; he suffered terribly, was in anguish; his moans wrung my heart. Everyone in the house was in alarm. Anna Fyodorovna kept praying that God would take him more quickly. They sent for the doctor. The doctor said that the patient would certainly die by the morning.

Old Pokrovsky spent the whole night in the passage at the door of his son's room; a rug of some sort was put down there for him. He kept coming into the room, it was dreadful to look at him. He was so crushed by sorrow that he seemed utterly senseless and without feeling. His head was shaking with terror. He was trembling all over and kept whispering something, talking about something to himself. It seemed to me he was going out of his mind.

Just before dawn the old man, worn out with mental suffering, fell asleep on his mat and slept like the dead. Between seven and eight his son began to die. I waked the father. Pokrovsky was fully conscious and said good-bye to us all. Strange! I could not cry, but my heart was torn to pieces.

But his last moments distressed and tortured me more than all. He kept asking for something at great length with his halting tongue and I could make out nothing from his words. My heart was lacerated! For a whole hour he was uneasy, kept grieving over something, trying to make some sign with his chill hands and then beginning pitifully to entreat me in his hoarse hollow voice; but his words were disconnected sounds and again I could make nothing of them. I brought everyone of the household to him, I gave him drink, but still he shook his head mournfully. At last I guessed what he wanted. He was begging me to draw up the window curtain and open the shutters. No doubt he wanted to look for the last time at the day, at God's light, at the sunshine. I drew back the curtain, but the dawning day was sad and melancholy as the poor failing life of the dying man. There was no sun. The clouds covered the sky with a shroud of mist; it was rainy, overcast, mournful. A fine rain was pattering on the window-panes and washing them with little rivulets of cold dirty water; it was dark and dingy. The pale daylight scarcely penetrated into the room and hardly rivalled the flickering flame of the little lamp lighted before the ikon. The dying man glanced at me mournfully, mournfully and shook his head; a minute later he died.

Anna Fyodorovna herself made the arrangements for the funeral. A coffin of the cheapest kind was bought and a carter was hired. To defray these expenses Anna Fyodorovna seized all Pokrovsky's books and other belongings. The old man argued with her, made a noise, took away all the books he could from her, stuffed his pockets full of them, put them in his hat, wherever he could, went about with them all those three days, and did not part with them even when he had to go to church. During those three days he seemed as it were, stupefied, as though he did not know what he was doing, and he kept fussing about the coffin with a strange solicitude; at one moment he set straight the wreath on his dead son and at the next he lighted and took away candles. It was evident that his thoughts could not rest on anything. Neither mother nor Anna Fyodorovna was at the funeral service at the church. Mother was ill; Anna Fyodorovna had got ready to go, but she quarrelled with old Pokrovsky and stayed behind. I went alone with the old man. During the service a terror came upon me—as though a foreboding of the future. I could scarcely stand up in church.

At last the coffin was closed, nailed up, put in the cart and taken away. I followed it only to the end of the street. The man drove at a trot. The old man ran after him, weeping loudly, his lamentations quivering and broken by his haste. The poor old man lost his hat and did not stop to pick it up. His head was drenched by the rain and the wind was rising; the sleet lashed and stung his face. The old man seemed not to feel the cold and wet and ran wailing from one side of the cart to the other, the skirts of his old coat fluttering in the wind like wings. Books were sticking out from all his pockets; in his hands was a huge volume which he held tightly. The passers-by took off their caps and crossed themselves. Some stopped and stood gazing in wonder at the poor old man. The books kept falling out of his pockets into the mud. People stopped him and pointed to what he had lost, he picked them up and fell to racing after the coffin again. At the corner of the street an old beggar woman joined him to follow the coffin with him. The cart turned the corner at last and disappeared from my sight. I went home. I threw myself on mother's bosom in terrible distress. I pressed her tightly in my arms, I kissed her and burst into floods of tears, huddling up to her fearfully as though trying to keep in my arms my last friend and not to give her up to death ... but death was already hovering over poor mother....

June 11.

How grateful I am to you for our walk yesterday to the Island, Makar Alexyevitch! How fresh and lovely it is there, how leafy and green! It's so long since I saw green leaves—when I was ill I kept fancying that I had to die and that I certainly should die—judge what must have been my sensations yesterday, how I must have felt ...

You must not be angry with me for having been so sad yesterday; I was very happy, very content, but in my very best moments I am always for some reason sad. As for my crying, that means nothing. I don't know myself why I am always crying. I feel ill and irritable; my sensations are due to illness. The pale cloudless sky, the sunset, the evening stillness—all that—I don't know—but I was somehow in the mood yesterday to take a dreary and miserable view of everything, so that my heart was too full and needed the relief of tears. But why am I writing all this to you? It is hard to make all that clear to one's own heart and still harder to convey it to another. But you, perhaps, will understand me. Sadness and laughter both at once! How kind you are really, Makar Alexyevitch! You looked into my eyes yesterday as though to read in them what I was feeling and were delighted with my rapture. Whether it was a bush, an avenue, a piece of water—you were there standing before me showing its beauties and peeping into my eyes as though you were displaying your possessions to me. That proves that you have a kind heart, Makar Alexyevitch. It's for that that I love you. Well, good-bye. I'm ill again to-day; I got my feet wet yesterday and have caught cold. Fedora is ailing, too, so now we are both on the sick list. Don't forget me. Come as often as you can.

Your V. D.

June 12.

MY DARLING VARVARA ALEXYEVNA,

Well, I had expected, my dear soul, that you would write me a description of our yesterday's expedition in a regular poem, and you have turned out nothing but one simple sheet. I say this because, though you wrote me so little in your sheet, yet you did describe it extraordinarily well and sweetly. The charms of nature, and the various rural scenes and all the rest about your feeling—in short, you described it all very well. Now I have no talent for it. If I smudge a dozen papers there's nothing to show for it; I can't describe anything. I have tried.

You write to me, my own, that I am a kind-hearted, good-natured man, incapable of injuring my neighbour, and able to understand the blessings of the Lord made manifest in nature, and you bestow various praises on me, in fact. All that is true, my darling, all that is perfectly true; I really am all that you say and I know it myself; but when one reads what you write one's heart is touched in spite of oneself and then all sorts of painful reflections come to one. Well, listen to me, Varinka dear, I will tell you something, my own.

I will begin with when I was only seventeen and went into the service, and soon the thirtieth year of my career there will be here. Well, I needn't say I have worn out many a uniform; I grew to manhood and to good sense and saw something of the world; I have lived, I may say, I have lived in the world so that on one occasion they even wanted to send up my name to receive a cross. Maybe you will not believe me, but I am really not lying. But there, my darling, in spite of everything, I have been badly treated by malicious people! I tell you, my own, that though I am an obscure person, a stupid person, perhaps, yet I have my feelings like anyone else. Do you know, Varinka, what a spiteful man did to me? I am ashamed to say what he has done to me; you will ask why did he do it? Why, because I am meek, because I am quiet, because I am good-natured! I did not suit their taste, so that's what brought it upon me. At first it began with, "You are this and that, Makar Alexyevitch," and then it came to saying, "It's no good asking Makar Alexyevitch!" And then it ended by, "Of course, that is Makar Alexyevitch!" You see, my precious, what a pass it came to; always Makar Alexyevitch to blame for everything; they managed to make Makar Alexyevitch a by-word all over the department, and it was not enough that they made me a by-word and almost a term of abuse, they attacked my boots, my uniform, my hair, my figure; nothing was to their taste, everything ought to be different! And all this has been repeated every blessed day from time immemorial. I am used to it, for I grow used to anything, because I am a meek man; but what is it all for? What harm do I do to anyone? Have I stolen promotion from anyone, or what? Have I blackened anyone's reputation with his superiors? Have I asked for anything extra out of turn? Have I got up some intrigue? Why, it's a sin for you to imagine such a thing, my dear soul! As though I could to anything of that sort! You've only to look at me, my own. Have I sufficient ability for intrigue and ambition? Then why have such misfortunes come upon me? God forgive me. Here you consider me a decent man, and you are ever so much better than any of them, my darling. Why, what is the greatest virtue in a citizen? A day or two ago, in private conversation, Yevstafy Ivanovitch said that the most important virtue in a citizen was to earn money. He said in jest (I know it was in jest) that morality consists in not being a burden to anyone. Well, I'm not a burden to anyone. My crust of bread is my own; it is true it is a plain crust of bread, at times a dry one; but there it is, earned by my toil and put to lawful and irreproachable use. Why, what can one do? I know very well, of course, that I don't do much by copying; but all the same I am proud of working and earning my bread in the sweat of my brow. Why, what if I am a copying clerk, after all? What harm is there in copying, after all? "He's a copying clerk," they say, but what is there discreditable in that? My handwriting is good, distinct and pleasant to the eye, and his Excellency is satisfied with it. I have no gift of language, of course, I know of myself that I haven't the confounded thing; that's why I have not got on in the service, and why even now, my own, I am writing to you simply, artlessly, just as the thought comes into my heart. . . . I know all that; but there, if everyone became an author, who would do the copying? I ask you that question and I beg you to answer it, Varinka dear. So I see now that I am necessary, that I am indispensable, and that it's no use to worry a man with nonsense. Well, let me be a rat if you like, since they see a resemblance! But the rat is necessary, but the rat is of service, but the rat is depended upon, but the rat is given a reward, so that's the sort of rat he is!

Enough about that subject though, my own! I did not intend to talk about that at all, but I got a little heated. Besides, it's pleasant from time to time to do oneself justice. Good-bye, my own, my darling, my kind comforter! I will come, I will certainly come to see you, my dearie, and meanwhile, don't be dull, I will bring you a book. Well, good-bye, then, Varinka.

Your devoted well-wisher,
MAKAR DYEVUSHKIN.

June 20.

DEAR SIR, MAKAR ALEXYEVITCH,

I write a hurried line, I am in haste, I have to finish my work up to time. You see, this is how it is: you can make a good bargain. Fedora says that a friend of hers has a uniform, quite new, underclothes, a waistcoat and cap, and all very cheap, they say; so you ought to buy them. You see, you are not badly off now, you say you have money; you say so yourself. Give over being so stingy, please. You know all those things are necessary. Just look at yourself, what old clothes you go about in. It's a disgrace! You're all in patches. You have no new clothes; I know that, though you declare that you have. God knows how you have managed to dispose of them. So do as I tell you, please buy these things. Do it for my sake; if you loved me, do it.

You sent me some linen as a present; but upon my word, Makar Alexyevitch, you are ruining yourself. It's no joke what you've spent on me, it's awful to think how much money! How fond you are of throwing away your money! I don't want it; it's all absolutely unnecessary. I know—I am convinced—that you love me. It is really unnecessary to remind me of it with presents; and it worries me taking them from you; I know what they cost you. Once for all, leave off, do you hear? I beg you, I beseech you. You ask me, Makar Alexyevitch, to send you the continuation of my diary, you want me to finish it. I don't know how what I have written came to be written! But I haven't the strength now to talk of my past; I don't even want to think of it; I feel frightened of those memories. To talk of my poor mother leaving her poor child to those monsters, too, is more painful than anything. My hearts throbs at the very thought of it: it is all still so fresh: I have not had time to think things over, still less to regain my calm, though it is all more than a year ago, now. But you know all that.

I've told you what Anna Fyodorovna thinks now; she blames me for ingratitude and repudiates all blame for her association with Mr. Bykov! She invites me to stay with her; she says that I am living on charity, that I am going to the bad. She says that if I go back to her she will undertake to set right everything with Mr. Bykov and compel him to make up for his behaviour to me. She says Mr. Bykov wants to give me a dowry. Bother them! I am happy here with you close by, with my kind Fedora whose devotion reminds me of my old nurse. Though you are only a distant relation you will protect me with your name. I don't know them. I shall forget them if I can. What more do they want of me? Fedora says that it is all talk, that they will leave me alone at last. God grant they may!

V. D.

June 21.

MY DARLING VARINKA,

I want to write, but I don't know how to begin. How strange it is, my precious, how we are living now. I say this because I have never spent my days in such joyfulness. Why, it is as though God had blessed me with a home and family of my own, my child, my pretty! But why are you making such a fuss about the four chemises I sent you? You needed them, you know—I found that out from Fedora. And it's a special happiness for me to satisfy your needs, Varinka, dear; it's my pleasure. You let me alone, my dear soul. Don't interfere with me and don't contradict me. I've never known anything like it, my darling. I've taken to going into society now. In the first place my life is twice as full; because you are living very near me and are a great comfort to me; and secondly, I have been invited to tea to-day by a lodger, a neighbour of mine, that clerk, Ratazyaev, who has the literary evenings. We meet this evening, we are going to read literature. So you see how we are getting on now, Varinka—you see! Well, good-bye. I've written all this for no apparent reason, simply to let you know of the affection I feel for you. You told Teresa to tell me, my love, that you want some silk for coloured embroidery. I will get you it, my darling, I will get the silk, I will get it. To-morrow I shall have the pleasure of satisfying you. I know where to buy it, too. And now I remain,

Your sincere friend,
MAKAR DYEVUSHKIN.

June 22.

DEAR MADAM, VARVARA ALEXYEVNA,

I must tell you, my own, that a very pitiful thing has happened in our flat, truly, truly, deserving of pity! Between four and five this morning Gorshkov's little boy died. I don't know what he died of. It seemed to be a sort of scarlatina, God only knows! I went to see these Gorshkovs. Oh, my dear soul, how poor they are! And what disorder! And no wonder; the whole family lives in one room, only divided by a screen for decency. There was a little coffin standing in the room already—a simple little coffin, but rather pretty; they bought it ready-made; the boy was nine years old, he was a promising boy, they say. But it was pitiful to look at them, Varinka! The mother did not cry, but she was so sad, so poor. And perhaps it will make it easier for them to have got one off their shoulders; but there are still two left, a baby, and a little girl, not much more than six. There's not much comfort really in seeing a child suffer, especially one's own little child, and having no means of helping him! The father was sitting in a greasy old dress suit on a broken chair. The tears were flowing from his eyes, but perhaps not from grief, but just the usual thing—his eyes are inflamed. He's such a strange fellow! He always turns red when you speak to him, gets confused and does not know what to answer. The little girl, their daughter, stood leaning against the coffin, such a poor little, sad, brooding child! And Varinka, my darling, I don't like it when children brood; it's painful to see! A doll made of rags was lying on the floor beside her; she did not play with it, she held her finger on her lips; she stood, without stirring. The landlady gave her a sweetmeat; she took it but did not eat it.

It was sad, Varinka, wasn't it?

MAKAR DYEVUSHKIN.

June 25.

DEAR MAKAR ALEXYEVITCH,

I am sending you back your book. A wretched, worthless little book not fit to touch! Where did you ferret out such a treasure? Joking apart, can you really like such a book, Makar Alexyevitch? I was promised the other day something to read. I will share it with you, if you like. And now good-bye. I really have not time to write more.

V. D.

June 26.

DEAR VARINKA,

The fact is that I really had not read that horrid book, my dear girl. It is true, I looked through it and saw it was nonsense, just written to be funny, to make people laugh; well, I thought, it really is amusing; maybe Varinka will like it, so I sent it you.

Now, Ratazyaev has promised to give me some real literature to read, so you will have some books, my darling. Ratazyaev knows, he's a connoisseur; he writes himself, ough, how he writes! His pen is so bold and he has a wonderful style, that is, there is no end to what there is in every word—in the most foolish ordinary vulgar word such as I might say sometimes to Faldoni or Teresa, even in such he has style. I go to his evenings. We smoke and he reads to us, he reads five hours at a stretch and we listen all the time. It's a perfect feast. Such charm, such flowers, simply flowers, you can gather a bouquet from each page! He is so affable, so kindly and friendly. Why, what am I beside him? What am I? Nothing. He is a man with a reputation, and what am I? I simply don't exist, yet he is cordial even to me. I am copying something for him. Only don't you imagine, Varinka, that there is something amiss in that, that he is friendly to me just because I am copying for him; don't you believe tittle-tattle, my dear girl, don't you believe worthless tittle-tattle. No, I am doing it of myself, of my own accord for his pleasure. I understand refinement of manners, my love; he is a kind, very kind man, and an incomparable writer.

Literature is a fine thing, Varinka, a very fine thing. I learnt that from them the day before yesterday. A profound thing, strengthening men's hearts, instructing them; there are all sorts of things written about that in their book. Very well written! Literature is a picture, that is, in a certain sense, a picture and a mirror: it's the passions, the expression, the subtlest criticism, edifying instruction and a document. I gathered all that from them. I tell you frankly, my darling, that one sits with them, one listens (one smokes a pipe like them, too, if you please), and when they begin to discuss and dispute about all sorts of matters, then I simply sit dumb; then, my dear soul, you and I can do nothing else but sit dumb. I am simply a blockhead, it seems. I am ashamed of myself, so that I try all the evening how to put in half a word in the general conversation, but there, as ill-luck would have it, I can't find that half word! And one is sorry for oneself, Varinka, that one is not this thing, nor that thing, that, as the saying is, "A man one is grown, but no mind of one's own." Why, what do I do in my free time now? I sleep like a fool! While instead of useless sleep I might have been busy in useful occupation; I might have sat down and writ- ten something that would have been of use to oneself and pleasant to others. Why, my dearie, you should only see what they get for it, God forgive them! Take Ratazyaev, for instance, what he gets. What is it for him to write a chapter? Why, sometimes he writes five in a day and he gets three hundred roubles a chapter. Some little anecdote, something curious—five hundred! take it or leave it, give it or be damned! Or another time, we'll put a thousand in our pocket! What do you say to that, Varvara Alexyevna? Why, he's got a little book of poems—such short poems—he's asking seven thousand, my dear girl, he's asking seven thousand; think of it! Why, it's real estate, it's house property! He says that they will give him five thousand, but he won't take it. I reasoned with him. I said, "Take five thousand for them, sir, and don't mind them. Why, five thousand's money!" "No," said he, "they'll give me seven, the swindlers!" He's a cunning fellow, really.

Well, my love, since we are talking of it I will copy a passage from the *Italian Passions* for you. That's the name of his book. Here, read it, Varinka, and judge for yourself. . . .

"Vladimir shuddered and his passion gurgled up furiously within him and his blood boiled. . . .

"'Countess,' he cried. 'Countess! Do you know how awful is this passion, how boundless this madness? No, my dreams did not deceive me! I love, I love ecstatically, furiously, madly! All your husband's blood would not quench the frantic surging ecstasy of my soul! A trivial obstacle cannot check the all-destroying, hellish fire that har- rows my exhausted breast. Oh, Zinaida, Zinaida!' . . .

"'Vladimir,' whispered the countess, beside herself, leaning on his shoulder. . . .

"'Zinaida!' cried the enraptured Smyelsky.

"His bosom exhaled a sigh. The fire flamed brightly on the altar of love and consumed the heart of the unhappy victims.

"'Vladimir,' the countess whispered, intoxicated. Her bosom heaved, her cheeks glowed crimson, her eyes glowed. . . .

"A new, terrible union was accomplished!

• • •

"Half an hour later the old count went into his wife's boudoir.

"'Well, my love, should we not order the samovar for our welcome guest?' he said, patting his wife on the cheek."

Well, I ask you, my dear soul, what do you think of it after that? It's true, it's a little free, there's no disputing that, but still it is fine. What is fine is fine! And now, if you will allow me, I will copy you another little bit from the novel *Yermak and Zuleika*.

You must imagine, my precious, that the Cossack, Yermak, the fierce and savage conqueror of Siberia, is in love with the daughter of Kutchum, the Tsar of Siberia, the Princess Zuleika, who has been taken captive by him. An episode straight from the times of Ivan the Terrible, as you see. Here is the conversation of Yermak and Zuleika.

"'You love me, Zuleika! Oh, repeat it, repeat it!' . . .

"'I love you, Yermak,' whispered Zuleika.

"'Heaven and earth, I thank you! I am happy! . . . You have given me everything, everything, for which my turbulent soul has striven from my boyhood's years. So it was to this thou hast led me, my guiding star, so it was for this thou hast led me here, beyond the Belt of Stone! I will show to all the world my Zuleika, and men, the frantic monsters, will not dare to blame me! Ah, if they could understand the secret sufferings of her tender soul, if they could see a whole poem in a tear of my Zuleika! Oh, let me dry that year with kisses, let me drink it up, that heavenly tear . . . unearthly one!'

"'Yermak,' said Zuleika, 'the world is wicked, men are unjust! They will persecute us, they will condemn us, my sweet Yermak! What is the poor maiden, nurtured amid the snows of Siberia in her father's *yurta* to do in your cold, icy, soulless, selfish world? People will not understand me, my desired one, my beloved one.'

"'Then will the Cossack's sabre rise up hissing about them.'"

And now, what do you say to Yermak, Varinka, when he finds out that his Zuleika has been murdered? . . . The blind old man, Kutchum, under cover of night steals into Yermak's tent in his absence and slays Zuleika, intending to deal a mortal blow at Yermak, who has robbed him of his sceptre and his crown.

"'Sweet is it to me to rasp the iron against the stone,' shouted Yermak in wild frenzy, whetting his knife of Damascus steel upon the magic stone; 'I'll have their blood, their blood! I will hack them! hack them! hack them to pieces!!!'"

And, after all that, Yermak, unable to survive his Zuleika, throws himself into the Irtish, and so it all ends.

And this, for instance, a tiny fragment written in a jocose style, simply to make one laugh.

"Do you know Ivan Prokofyevitch Yellow-paunch? Why, the man who bit Prokofy Ivanovitch's leg. Ivan Prokofyevitch is a man of hasty temper, but, on the other hand, of rare virtues; Prokofy Ivanovitch, on the other hand, is extremely fond of a rarebit on toast. Why, when Pelagea Antonovna used to know him . . . Do you know Pelagea Antonovna? the woman who always wears her petticoat inside out."

That's humour, you know, Varinka, simply humour. He rocked with laughter when he read us that. He *is* a fellow, God forgive him! But though it's rather jocose and very playful, Varinka dear, it is quite innocent, without the slightest trace of free-thinking or liberal ideas. I must observe, my love, that Ratazyaev is a very well-behaved man and so an excellent author, not like other authors.

And, after all, an idea sometimes comes into one's head, you know. . . . What if I were to write something, what would happen then? Suppose that, for instance, apropos of nothing, there came into the world a book with the title—*Poems by Makar Dyevushkin?* What would my little angel say then? How does that strike you? What do you think of it? And I can tell you, my darling, that as soon as my book came out, I certainly should not dare to show myself in the Nevsky Prospect. Why, how should I feel when everyone would be saying, Here comes the author and poet, Dyevushkin? There's Dyevushkin himself, they would say! What should I do with my boots then? They are, I may mention in passing, my dear girl, almost always covered with patches, and the soles too, to tell the truth, sometimes break away in a very unseemly fashion. What should we do when everyone knew that the author Dyevushkin had patches on his boots! Some countess or duchess would hear of it, and what would she say, the darling? Perhaps she would not notice it; for I imagine countesses don't trouble themselves about boots, especially clerks' boot (for you know there are boots and boots), but they would tell her all about it, her friends would give me away. Ratazyaev, for instance, would be the first to give me away; he visits the Countess V.; he says that he goes to all her receptions, and he's quite at home there. He says she is such a darling, such a literary lady, he says. He's a rogue, that Ratazyaev!

But enough of that subject; I write all this for fun, my little angel, to amuse you. Good-bye, my darling, I have scribbled you a lot of nonsense, but that is just because I am in a very good humour to-day. We all dined together to-day at Ratazyaev's (they are rogues, Varinka dear), and brought out such a cordial. . . .

But there, why write to you about that! Only mind you don't imagine anything about me, Varinka. I don't mean anything by it. I will send you the books, I will certainly send them. . . . One of Paul de Kock's novels is being passed round from one to another, but Paul de Kock will not do for you, my precious. . . . No, no! Paul de Kock won't do for you. They say of him, Varinka dear, that he rouses all the Petersburg critics to righteous indignation. I send you a pound of sweetmeats—I bought them on purpose for you. Do you hear, darling? think of me at every sweetmeat. Only don't nibble up the sugar-candy but only suck it, or you will get toothache. And perhaps you like candied peel?——write and tell me. Well, good-bye, good-bye. Christ be with you, my darling!

I remain ever,
Your most faithful friend,
Makar Dyevushkin.

June 27.

Dear Sir, Makar Alexyevitch,

Fedora tells me that, if I like, certain people will be pleased to interest themselves in my position, and will get me a very good position as a governess in a family. What do you think about it, my friend—shall I go, or shall I not? Of course I should not then be a burden upon you, and the situation seems a good one; but, on the other hand, I feel somehow frightened at going into a strange house. They are people with an estate in the country. When they want to know all about me, when they begin asking questions, making inquiries—why, what should I say then?—besides, I am so shy and unsociable, I like to go on living in the corner I am used to. It's better somehow where one is used to being; even though one spends half one's time grieving, still it is better. Besides, it means leaving Petersburg; and God knows what my duties will be, either; perhaps they will simply make me look after the children, like a nurse. And they are such queer people, too; they've had three governesses already in two years. Do advise me, Makar Alexyevitch, whether to go or not. And why do you never come and see me? You hardly ever show your face, we scarcely ever meet except on Sundays at mass. What an unsociable person you are! You are as bad as I am! And you know I am almost a relation. You don't love me, Makar Alexyevitch, and I am sometimes very sad all alone. Sometimes, especially when it is getting dark, one sits all alone. Fedora goes off somewhere, one sits and sits and thinks—one remembers all the past, joyful and sad alike—it all passes before one's eyes, it all rises up as though out of a mist. Familiar faces appear (I am almost beginning to see them in reality)—I see mother most often of all . . . And what dreams I have! I feel that I am not at all well, I am so weak; to-day, for instance, when I got out of bed this morning, I turned giddy; and I have such a horrid cough, too! I feel, I know, that I shall soon die. Who will bury me? Who will follow my coffin! Who will grieve for me! . . . And perhaps I may have to die in a strange place, in a strange house! . . . My goodness! how sad life is, Makar Alexyevitch. Why do you keep feeding me on sweetmeats? I really don't know where you get so much money from? Ah, my friend, take care of your money, for God's sake, take care of it. Fedora is selling the cloth rug I have embroidered; she is getting fifty paper roubles for it. That's very good, I thought it would be less. I shall give Fedora three silver roubles, and shall get a new dress for myself, a plain one but warm. I shall make you a waistcoat, I shall make it myself, and I shall choose a good material.

Fedora got me a book, *Byelkin's Stories,* which I will send you, if you care to read it. Only don't please keep it, or make it dirty, it belongs to someone else—it's one of Pushkin's works. Two years ago I read these stories with my mother. And it was so sad for me now to read them over again. If you have any books send them to me—only not if you get them from Ratazyaev. He will certainly lend you his books if he has ever published anything. How do you like his works, Makar Alexyevitch? Such nonsense . . . Well, good-bye! How I have been chattering! When I am sad I am glad to chatter about anything. It does me good; at once one feels better, especially if one expresses all that lies in one's heart. Good-bye. Good-bye, my friend!

Your

V. D.

June 28.

MY PRECIOUS VARVARA ALEXYEVNA,

Leave off worrying yourself, I wonder you are not ashamed. Come, give over, my angel! How is it such thoughts come into your mind? You are not ill, my love, you are not ill at all; you are blooming, you are really blooming; a little pale, but still blooming. And what do you mean by these dreams, these visions? For shame, my darling, give over; you must simply laugh at them. Why do I sleep well? Why is nothing wrong with me? You should look at me, my dear soul. I get along all right, I sleep quietly, I am as healthy and hearty as can be, a treat to look at. Give over, give over, darling, for shame. You must reform. I know your little ways, my dearie; as soon as any trouble comes, you begin fancying things and worrying about something. For my sake give over, my darling. Go into a family?—Never! No, no, no, and what notion is this of yours? What is this idea that has come over you? And to leave Petersburg too. No, my darling, I won't allow it. I will use every means in my power to oppose such a plan. I'll sell my old coat and walk about the street in my shirt before you shall want for anything. No, Varinka, no, I know you! It's folly, pure folly. And there is no doubt that it is all Fedora's fault: she's evidently a stupid woman, she puts all these ideas into your head. Don't you trust her, my dear girl. You probably don't know everything yet, my love. . . . She's a silly woman, discontented and nonsensical; she worried her husband out of his life. Or perhaps she has vexed you in some way? No, no, my precious, not for anything! And what would become of me then, what would there be left for me to do? No, Varinka darling, you put that out of your little head. What is there wanting in your life with us? We can never rejoice enough over you, you love us, so do go on living here quietly. Sew or read, or don't sew if you like—it does not matter—only go on living with us or, only think yourself, why, what would it be like without you? . . .

Here, I will get you some books and then maybe we'll go for a walk somewhere again. Only you must give over, my dearie, you must give over. Pull yourself together and don't be foolish over trifles! I'll come and see you and very soon too. Only accept what I tell you plainly and candidly about it; you are wrong, my darling, very wrong. Of course, I am an ignorant man and I know myself that I am ignorant, that I have hardly a ha'porth of education. But that's not what I am talking about, and I'm not what matters, but I will stand up for Ratazyaev, say what you like. He writes well, very, very well, and I say it again, he writes very well. I don't agree with you and I never can agree with you. It's written in a flowery abrupt style, with figures of speech. There are ideas of all sorts in it, it is very good! Perhaps you read it without feeling, Varinka; you were out of humour when you read it, vexed with Fedora, or something had gone wrong. No, you read it with feeling; best when you are pleased and happy and in a pleasant humour, when, for instance, you have got a sweetmeat in your mouth, that's when you must read it. I don't dispute (who denies it?) that there are better writers than Ratazyaev, and very much better in fact, but they are good and Ratazyaev is good too. He writes in his own special way, and does very well to write. Well, good-bye, my precious, I can't write more;

I must make haste, I have work to do. Mind now, my love, my precious little dearie; calm yourself, and God will be with you, and I remain your faithful friend,

MAKAR DYEVUSHKIN.

P.S.—Thanks for the book, my own; we will read Pushkin too, and this evening I shall be sure to come and see you.

MY DEAR MAKAR ALEXYEVITCH,

No, my friend, no, I ought not to go on living among you. On second thoughts I consider that I am doing very wrong to refuse such a good situation. I shall have at least my daily bread secure; I will do my best, I will win the affection of the strangers, I will even try to overcome my defects, if necessary. Of course it is painful and irksome to live with strangers, to try and win their good-will, to hide one's feelings, and suppress oneself, but God will help me. I mustn't be a recluse all my life. I have had experiences like it before. I remember when I was a little thing and used to go to school. I used to be frolicking and skipping about all Sundays at home; sometimes mother would scold me—but nothing mattered, my heart was light and my soul was full of joy all the while. As evening approached an immense sadness would come over me—at nine o'clock I had to go back to school, and there it was all cold, strange, severe, the teachers were so cross on Mondays, one had such a pain at one's heart, one wanted to cry; one would go into a corner and cry all alone, hiding one's tears—they would say one was lazy; and I wasn't crying in the least because I had to do my lessons.

But, after all, I got used to it, and when I had to leave school I cried also when I said good-bye to my schoolfellows. And I am not doing right to go on being a burden to both of you. That thought is a torment to me. I tell you all this openly because I am accustomed to be open with you. Do you suppose I don't see how early Fedora gets up in the morning, and sets to work at her washing and works till late at night?—and old bones want rest. Do you suppose I don't see how you are ruining yourself over me, and spending every halfpenny? You are not a man of property, my friend! You tell me that you will sell your last rag before I shall want for anything. I believe you, my friend, I trust your kind heart, but you say that now. Now you have money you did not expect, you've received something extra, but later on? You know yourself, I am always ill; and I can't work like you, though I should be heartily glad to, and one does not always get work. What is left for me? To break my heart with grief looking at you two dear ones. In what way can I be of the slightest use to you? And why am I so necessary to you, my friend? What good have I done you? I am only devoted to you with my whole soul, I love you warmly, intensely, with my whole heart, but—my fate is a bitter one! I know how to love and I can love, but I can do nothing to repay you for your kindness. Don't dissuade me any more, think it over and tell me your final opinion. Meanwhile I remain your loving,

V. D.

July 1.

Nonsense, nonsense, Varinka, simply nonsense! Let you alone and there's no knowing what notion you will take into your little head. One thing's not right and another thing's not right. And I see now that it is all nonsense. And what more do you want, my dear girl? just tell me that! We love you, you love us, we're all contented and happy— what more do you want? And what will you do among strangers? I expect you don't know yet what strangers are like . . . You had better ask me and I will tell you what strangers are like. I know them, my darling, I know them very well, I've had to eat their bread. They are spiteful, Varinka, spiteful; so spiteful that you would have no heart left, they would torment it so with reproach, upbraiding and ill looks. You are snug and happy among us as though you were in a little nest; besides, we shall feel as though we had lost our head when you are gone; why, what can we do without you; what is an old man like me to do then? You are no use to us? No good to us? How no good? Come, my love, think yourself how much good you are! You are a great deal of good to me, Varinka. You have such a good influence . . . Here I am thinking about you now and I am happy . . . Sometimes I write you a letter and put all my feelings into it and get a full answer to everything back from you. I bought you a little wardrobe, got you a hat; some commission comes from you; I carry out the commission . . . How can you say, you are no use to me? And what should I be good for in my old age? Perhaps you have not thought of that, Varinka, that's just what you had better think about, "what will he be good for without me?" I am used to you, my darling. Or else what will come of it? I shall go straight to the Neva, and that will be the end of it. Yes, really, Varinka, that will be the only thing left for me to do when you are gone. Ah, Varinka, my darling. It seems you want me to be taken to Volkovo Cemetery in a common cart; with only an old draggletail beggar-woman to follow me to the grave; you want them to throw the earth upon me and go away and leave me alone. It's too bad, too bad, my dear! It's sinful really, upon my word it's a sin! I send you back your book, Varinka, my darling, and if you ask my opinion about your book, dear, I must say that never in my life have I read such a splendid book. I wonder now, my darling, how I can have lived till now such an ignoramus, God forgive me! What have I been doing? What backwoods have I been brought up in? Why, I know nothing, my dear girl; why, I know absolutely nothing. I know nothing at all. I tell you, Varinka, plainly— I'm a man of no education: I have read little hitherto—very little, scarcely anything: I have read *The Picture of Man,* a clever work; I have read *The boy who played funny tunes on the bells* and *The Cranes of Ibicus*; that's all, and I never read anything else. Now I have read *The Stationmaster* in your book; let me tell you, my darling, it happens that one goes on living, and one does not know that there is a book there at one's side where one's whole life is set forth, as though it were reckoned upon one's fingers. And what one never so much as guessed before, when one begins reading such a book one remembers little by little and guesses and discovers. And this is another reason why I like your book: one sometimes reads a book, whatever it may be, and you can't for the life of you understand it, it's so deep. I, for instance, am stupid, I'm stupid by nature, so I can't read very serious books; but I read this as though I had written it myself, as though I had taken my own heart, just as it is, and turned it inside out before people and described it in detail, that's what it is like. And it's a simple subject, my goodness, yet what a thing it is! Really it is just as I should have described it; why not describe it? You know I feel exactly the same as in the book, and I have been at times in exactly the same positions as, for instance, that Samson Vyrin, poor fellow. And how many Samson Vyrins are going about amongst us, poor dears! And how clearly it is all described! Tears almost started into my eyes when I read that the poor sinner took to drink, became such a drunkard that he lost his senses and slept the whole day under a sheepskin coat and drowned his grief in punch, and wept piteously, wiping his eyes with the dirty skirt of his coat when he thought of his lost lamb, his daughter Dunyasha. Yes, it's natural. You should read it, it's natural. It's living! I've seen it myself; it's all about me; take Teresa, for instance—but why go so far? Take our poor clerk, for instance—Why, he is perhaps just a Samson Vyrin, only he has another surname, Gorshkov. It's the general lot, Varinka dear, it might happen to you or to me. And the count who lives on the Nevsky on the riverside, he would be just the same, it would only seem different because everything there is done in their own way, in style, yet he would be just the same, anything may happen, and the same thing may happen to me. That's the truth of the matter, my darling, and yet you want to go away from us; it's a sin, Varinka, it may be the end of me. You may be the ruin of yourself and me too, my own. Oh, my little dearie, for God's sake put out of your little head all these wilful ideas and don't torment me for nothing. How can you keep yourself, my weak little unfledged bird? How can you save yourself from ruin, protect yourself from villains? Give over, Varinka, think better of it; don't listen to nonsensical advice and persuasion, and read your book again, read it with attention; that will do you good.

I talked of *The Stationmaster* to Ratazyaev. He told me that that was all old-fashioned and that now books with pictures and descriptions have all come in; I really did not quite understand what he said about it. He ended by saying that Pushkin is fine and that he is a glory to holy Russia, and he said a great deal more to me about him. Yes, it's good, Varinka, very good; read it again with attention; follow my advice, and make an old man happy by your obedience. Then God Himself will reward you, my own, He will certainly reward you.

Your sincere friend,
MAKAR DYEVUSHKIN.

DEAR SIR, MAKAR DYEVUSHKIN,

Fedora brought me fifteen silver roubles to-day. How pleased she was, poor thing, when I gave her three! I write to you in haste. I am now cutting you out a waistcoat—it's charming material—yellow with flowers on it. I send you a book: there are all sorts of stories in it; I have read some of them, read the one called *The Cloak*. You persuade me to go to the theatre with you; wouldn't it be expensive? Perhaps we could go to the gallery somewhere. It's a long while since I've been to the theatre, in fact I can't remember when I went. Only I'm afraid whether such a treat would not cost too much? Fedora simply shakes her head. She says that you have begun to live beyond your means and I see how much you spend, on me alone! Mind, my friend, that you don't get into difficulties. Fedora tells me of rumours—that you have had a quarrel with your landlady for not paying your rent; I am very anxious about you. Well, good-bye, I'm in a hurry. It's a trifling matter, I'm altering a ribbon on a hat.

P.S.—You know, if we go to the theatre, I shall wear my new hat and my black mantle. Will that be all right?

July 7.

DEAR MADAM, VARVARA ALEXYEVNA,

. . . So I keep thinking about yesterday. Yes, my dear girl, even we have had our follies in the past. I fell in love with that actress, I fell head over ears in love with her, but that was nothing. The strangest thing was that I had scarcely seen her at all, and had only been at the

theatre once, and yet for all that I fell in love. There lived next door
to me five noisy young fellows. I got to know them, I could not help
getting to know them, though I always kept at a respectable distance
from them. But not to be behind them I agreed with them in everything. They talked to me about this actress. Every evening as soon as
the theatre was opened, the whole company—they never had a halfpenny for necessities—the whole party set off to the theatre to the
gallery and kept clapping and clapping, and calling, calling for that
actress—they were simply frantic! And after that they would not let
one sleep; they would talk about her all night without ceasing, everyone called her his Glasha, everyone of them was in love with her, they
all had the same canary in their hearts. They worked me up: I was a
helpless youngster then. I don't know how I came to go, but one
evening I found myself in the fourth gallery with them. As for seeing,
I could see nothing more than the corner of the curtain, but I heard
everything. The actress certainly had a pretty voice—a musical voice
like a nightingale, as sweet as honey; we all clapped our hands and
shouted and shouted, we almost got into trouble, one was actually
turned out. I went home. I walked along as though I were drunk! I
had nothing left in my pocket but one silver rouble, and it was a good
ten days before I could get my salary. And what do you think, my
love? Next day before going to the office I went to a French per-
fumer's and spent my whole fortune on perfume and scented soap—
I really don't know why I bought all that. And I did not dine at home
but spent the whole time walking up and down outside her window.
She lived in Nevsky Prospect on the fourth storey. I went home for
an hour or so, rested, and out into the Nevsky again, simply to pass by
her windows. For six weeks I used to walk to and fro like that and
hang about her; I was constantly hiring smart sledges and kept driving
about so as to pass her window: I ruined myself completely, ran into
debt, and then got over my passion, I got tired of it. So you see, my
precious, what an actress can make of a respectable man! I was a
youngster though, I was a youngster then! . . .

M. D.

July 8.

Dear Madam, Varvara Alexyevna,

I hasten to return you the book you lent me on the sixth of this
month, and therewith I hasten to discuss the matter with you. It's
wrong of you, my dear girl, it's wrong of you to put me to the necessity of it. Allow me to tell you, my good friend, every position in the
lot of man is ordained by the Almighty. One man is ordained to wear

the epaulettes of a general, while it is another's lot to serve as a titular councillor; it is for one to give commands, for another to obey without repining, in fear and humility. It is in accordance with man's capacities; one is fit for one thing and one for another, and their capacities are ordained by God himself. I have been nearly thirty years in the service; my record is irreproachable; I have been sober in my behaviour, and I have never had any irregularity put down to me. As a citizen I look upon myself in my own mind as having my faults, but my virtues, too. I am respected by my superiors, and His Excellency himself is satisfied with me; and though he has not so far shown me any special marks of favour, yet I know that he is satisfied. My handwriting is fairly legible and good, not too big and not too small, rather in the style of italics, but in any case satisfactory; there is no one among us except, perhaps, Ivan Prokofyevitch who writes as well. I am old and my hair is grey; that's the only fault I know of in me. Of course, there is no one without his little failings. We're all sinners, even you are a sinner, my dear! But no serious offence, no impudence has ever been recorded against me, such as anything against the regulations, or any disturbance of public tranquillity; I have never been noticed for anything like that, such a thing has never happened—in fact, I almost got a decoration, but what's the use of talking! You ought to have known all that, my dear, and he ought to have known; if a man undertakes to write he ought to know all about it. No, I did not expect this from you, my dear girl, no, Varinka! You are the last person from whom I should have expected it.

What! So now you can't live quietly in your own little corner—whatever it may be like—not stirring up any mud, as the saying is, interfering with no one, knowing yourself, and fearing God, without people's interfering with you, without their prying into your little den and trying to see what sort of life you lead at home, whether for instance you have a good waistcoat, whether you have all you ought to have in the way of underclothes, whether you have boots and what they are lined with; what you eat, what you drink, what you write? And what even if I do sometimes walk on tiptoe to save my boots where the pavement's bad? Why write of another man that he sometimes goes short, that he has no tea to drink, as though everyone is always bound to drink tea—do I look into another man's mouth to see how he chews his crust, have I ever insulted anyone in that way? No, my dear, why insult people, when they are not interfering with you! Look here, Varvara Alexyevna, this is what it comes to: you work, and work regularly and devotedly; and your superiors respect you (however things may be, they do respect you), and here under your very nose, for no apparent reason, neither with your leave nor by your leave, somebody makes a caricature of you. Of course one does sometimes get something new—and is so pleased that one lies awake thinking about it, one is so pleased, one puts on new boots for instance, with such enjoyment; that is true: I have felt it because it is pleasant to see one's foot in a fine smart boot—that's truly described! But I am really surprised that Fyodor Fyodorovitch should have let such a book pass without notice and without defending himself. It is true that, though he is a high official, he is young and likes at times to make his voice heard. Why shouldn't he make his voice heard, why not give us a scolding if we need it? Scold to keep up the tone of the office, for instance—well, he must, to keep up the tone; you must teach men, you must give them a good talking to; for, between ourselves, Varinka, we clerks do nothing without a good talking to. Everyone is only on the look-out to get off somewhere, so as to say, I was sent here or there, and to avoid work and edge out of it. And as there are various grades in the service and as each grade requires a special sort of reprimand corresponding to the grade, it's natural that the tone of the reprimand should differ in the various grades—that's in the order of things—why, the whole world rests on that, my dear soul, on our all keeping up our authority with one another, on each one of us scolding the other. Without that precaution, the world could not go on and there would be no sort of order. I am really surprised that Fyodor Fyodorovitch let such an insult pass without attention. And why write such things? And what's the use of it? Why, will someone who reads it order me a cloak because of it; will he buy me new boots? No, Varinka, he will read it and ask for a contribution. One hides oneself sometimes, one hides oneself, one tries to conceal one's weak points, one's afraid to show one's nose at times anywhere because one is afraid of tittle-tattle, because they can work up a tale against you about anything in the world—anything. And here now all one's private and public life is being dragged into literature, it is all printed, read, laughed and gossiped about! Why, it will be impossible to show oneself in the street. It's all so plainly told, you know, that one might be recognised in one's walk. To be sure, it's as well that he does make up for it a little at the end, that he does soften it a bit, that after that passage when they throw the papers at his head, it does put in, for instance, that for all that he was a conscientious man, a good citizen, that he did not deserve such treatment from his fellow-clerks, that he respected his elders (his example might be followed, perhaps, in that), had no ill-will against anyone, believed in God and died (if he will have it that he died) regretted. But it would have been better not to let him die, poor fellow, but to make the coat be found, to make Fyodor Fyodorovitch—what am I saying? I mean, make that general, finding out his good qualities, question him in his office, promote him in his office, and give him a good increase in his salary, for then, you see, wickedness would have been punished, and virtue would have been triumphant, and his fellow-clerks would have got nothing by it. I should have done that, for instance, but as it is, what is there special about it, what is there good in it? It's just an insignificant example from vulgar, everyday life. And what induced you to send me such a book, my own? Why, it's a book of an evil tendency, Varinka, it's untrue to life, for there cannot have been such a clerk. No, I must make a complaint, Varinka. I must make a formal complaint.

Your very humble servant,
MAKAR DYEVUSHKIN.

July 27.

DEAR SIR, MAKAR ALEXYEVITCH,

Your latest doings and letters have frightened, shocked, and amazed me, and what Fedora tells me has explained it all. But what reason had you to be so desperate and to sink to such a depth as you have sunk to, Makar Alexyevitch? Your explanation has not satisfied me at all. Isn't it clear that I was right in trying to insist on taking the situation that was offered me? Besides, my last adventure has thoroughly frightened me. You say that it's your love for me that makes you keep in hiding from me. I saw that I was deeply indebted to you while you persuaded me that you were only spending your savings on me, which you said you had lying by in the bank in case of need. Now, when I learn that you had no such money at all, but, hearing by chance of my straitened position, and touched by it, you actually spent your salary, getting it in advance, and even sold your clothes when I was ill—now that I have discovered all this I am put in such an agonising position that I still don't know how to take it, and what to think about it. Oh, Makar Alexyevitch! You ought to have confined yourself to that first kind help inspired by sympathy and the feeling of kinship and not have wasted money afterwards on luxuries. You have been false to our friendship, Makar Alexyevitch, for you weren't open with me. And now, when I see that you were spending your last penny on finery, on sweetmeats, on excursions, on the theatre and on books—now I am paying dearly for all that in regret for my frivolity (for I took it all from you without troubling myself about you); and everything with which you tried to give me pleasure is now turned to grief for me, and has left nothing but useless regret. I have noticed your depression of late, and, although I was nervously apprehensive of some trouble, what has happened never entered my head. What! Could you lose heart so completely, Makar Alexyevitch! Why, what am I to think of you now, what will everyone who knows you say of you now? You, whom I always respected for your good heart, your discretion, and your good sense. You have suddenly given way to such a revolting vice, of which one saw no sign in you before. What were my feelings when Fedora told me you were found in the street in a state of inebriety, and were brought home to your lodgings by the police! I was petrified with amazement, though I did expect something extraordinary, as there had been no sign of you for four days. Have you thought, Makar Alexyevitch, what your chiefs at the office will say when they learn the true cause of your absence? You say that everyone laughs at you, that they all know of our friendship, and that your neighbours speak of me in their jokes, too. Don't pay any attention to that, Makar Alexyevitch, and for goodness' sake, calm yourself. I am alarmed about your affair with those officers, too; I have heard a vague account of it. Do explain what it all means. You write that you were afraid to tell me, that you were afraid to lose my affection by your confession, that you were in despair, not knowing how to help me in my illness, that you sold everything to keep me and prevent my going to hospital, that you got into debt as far as you possibly could, and have unpleasant scenes every day with your landlady—but you made a mistake in concealing all this from me. Now I know it all, however. You were reluctant to make me realise that I was the cause of your unhappy position, and now you have caused me twice as much grief by your behaviour. All this has shocked me, Makar Alexyevitch. Oh, my dear friend! misfortune is an infectious disease, the poor and unfortunate ought to avoid one another, for fear of making each other worse. I have brought you trouble such as you knew nothing of in your old humble and solitary existence. All this is distressing and killing me.

Write me now openly all that happened to you and how you came to behave like that. Set my mind at rest if possible. It isn't selfishness makes me write to you about my peace of mind, but my affection and love for you, which nothing will ever efface from my heart. Goodbye. I await your answer with impatience. You had a very poor idea of me, Makar Alexyevitch.

Your loving

VARVARA DOBROSELOV.

June 28.

MY PRECIOUS VARVARA ALEXYEVNA—

Well, as now everything is over and, little by little, things are beginning to be as they used to be, again let me tell you one thing, my good friend: you are worried by what people will think about me, to which I hasten to assure you, Varvara Alexyevna, that my reputation is dearer to me than anything. For which reason and with reference to my misfortunes and all those disorderly proceedings I beg to inform you that no one of the authorities at the office know anything about it or will know anything about it. So that they will all feel the same respect for me as before. The one thing I'm afraid of is gossip. At home our landlady did nothing but shout, and now that with the help of your ten roubles I have paid part of what I owe her she does nothing more than grumble; as for other people, they don't matter, one mustn't borrow money of them, that's all, and to conclude my explanations I tell you, Varvara Alexyevna, that your respect for me I esteem more highly than anything on earth, and I am comforted by it now in my temporary troubles. Thank God that the first blow and the first shock are over and that you have taken it as you have, and don't look on me as a false friend, or an egoist for keeping you here and deceiving you because I love you as my angel and could not bring myself to part from you. I've set to work again assiduously and have begun performing my duties well. Yevstafy Ivanovitch did just say a word when I passed him by yesterday. I will not conceal from you, Varinka, that I am overwhelmed by my debts and the awful condition of my wardrobe, but that again does not matter, and about that too, I entreat you, do not despair, my dear. Send me another half rouble. Varinka, that half rouble rends my heart too. So that's what it has come to now, that is how it is, old fool that I am; it's not I helping you, my angel, but you, my poor little orphan, helping me. Fedora did well to get the money. For the time I have no hopes of getting any, but if there should be any prospects I will write to you fully about it all. But gossip, gossip is what I am most uneasy about. I kiss your little hand and implore you to get well. I don't write more fully because I am in haste to get to the office. For I want by industry and assiduity to atone for all my shortcomings in the way of negligence in the office; a further account of all that happened and my adventures with the officers I put off till this evening.

Your respectful and loving
MAKAR DYEVUSHKIN.

July 28.

MY PRECIOUS VARINKA—

Ach, Varinka, Varinka! This time the sin is on your side and your conscience. You completely upset and perplexed me by your letter, and only now, when at my leisure I looked into the inmost recesses of my heart, I saw that I was right, perfectly right. I am not talking of my drinking (that's enough of it, my dear soul, that's enough) but about my loving you and that I was not at all unreasonable in loving you, not at all unreasonable. You know nothing about it, my darling; why, if only you knew why it all was, why I was bound to love you, you wouldn't talk like that. All your reasoning about it is only talk, and I am sure that in your heart you feel quite differently.

My precious, I don't even know myself and don't remember what happened between me and the officers. I must tell you, my angel, that up to that time I was in the most terrible perturbation. Only imagine! for a whole month I had been clinging to one thread, so to say. My position was most awful. I was concealing it from you, and concealing it at home too. But my landlady made a fuss and a clamour. I should not have minded that. The wretched woman might have clamoured but, for one thing, it was the disgrace and, for another, she had found out about our friendship—God knows how—and was making such talk about it all over the house that I was numb with horror and put wool in my ears, but the worst of it is that other people did not put wool in theirs, but pricked them up, on the contrary. Even now I don't know where to hide myself. . . .

Well, my angel, all this accumulation of misfortunes of all sorts overwhelmed me utterly. Suddenly I heard a strange thing from Fedora: that a worthless profligate had called upon you and had insulted you by dishonourable proposals; that he did insult you, insult you deeply, I can judge from myself, my darling, for I was deeply insulted myself. That crushed me, my angel, that overwhelmed me and made me lose my head completely. I ran out, Varinka dear, in unutterable fury. I wanted to go straight to him, the reprobate. I did not know what I meant to do. I won't have you insulted, my angel! Well, I was sad! And at that time it was raining, sleet was falling, it was horribly wretched! . . . I meant to turn back. . . . Then came my downfall. I met Emelyan Ilyitch—he is a clerk, that is, was a clerk, but he is not a clerk now because he was turned out of our office. I don't know what he does now, he just hangs about there. Well, I went with him. Then—but there, Varinka, will it amuse you to read about your friend's misfortunes, his troubles, and the story of the trials he has endured? Three days later that Emelyan egged me on and I went to see him, that officer. I got his address from our porter. Since we are talking about it, my dear, I noticed that young gallant long ago: I kept an eye upon him when he lodged in our buildings. I see now that what I did was unseemly, because I was not myself when I was shown up to him. Truly, Varinka, I don't remember anything about it, all I remember is that there were a great many officers with him, else I was seeing double—goodness knows. I don't remember what

I said either, I only know that I said a great deal in my honest indignation. But then they turned me out, then they threw me downstairs—
that is, not really threw me downstairs, but turned me out. You know
already, Varinka, how I returned: that's the whole story. Of course I lowered myself and my reputation has suffered, but, after all, no one knows
of it but you, no outsider knows of it, and so it is all as though it had
never happened. Perhaps that is so, Varinka, what do you think? The
only thing is, I know for a fact that last year Aksenty Osipovitch in the
same way assaulted Pyotr Petrovitch but in secret, he did it in secret. He
called him into the porter's room—I saw it all through the crack in the
door—and there he settled the matter, as was fitting, but in a gentlemanly way, for no one saw it except me, and I did not matter—that is,
I did not tell anyone. Well, after that Pyotr Petrovitch and Aksenty
Osipovitch were all right together. Pyotr Petrovitch, you know, is a man
with self-respect, so he told no one, so that now they even bow and
shake hands. I don't dispute, Varinka, I don't venture to dispute with
you all that I have degraded myself terribly, and, what is worst of all, I
have lowered myself in my own opinion, but no doubt it was destined
from my birth, no doubt it was my fate, and there's no escaping one's
fate, you know.

Well, that is an exact account of my troubles and misfortunes,
Varinka, all of them, things such that reading of them is unprofitable.
I am very far from well, Varinka, and have lost all the playfulness of
my feelings. Herewith I beg to testify to my devotion, love and
respect. I remain, dear madam, Varvara Alexyevna,

Your humble servant,
Makar Dyevushkin.

July 29.

My dear Makar Alexyevitch!

I have read your two letters, and positively groaned! Listen, my
dear; you are either concealing something from me and have written
to me only part of all your troubles, or . . . really, Makar Alexyevitch,
there is a touch of incoherency about your letters still. . . . Come and
see me, for goodness' sake, come to-day; and listen, come straight to
dinner, you know I don't know how you are living, or how you have
managed about your landlady. You write nothing about all that, and
your silence seems intentional. So, good-bye, my friend; be sure and
come to us to-day; and you would do better to come to us for dinner
every day. Fedora cooks very nicely. Good-bye.

Your
Varvara Dobroselov.

MY DEAR VARVARA ALEXYEVNA,—

You are glad, my dear girl, that God has sent you a chance to do
one good turn for another and show your gratitude to me. I believe
that, Varinka, and I believe in the goodness of your angelic heart, and
I am not saying it to reproach you—only do not upbraid me for being
a spendthrift in my old age. Well, if I have done wrong, there's no help
for it; only to hear it from you, my dearie, is very bitter! Don't be
angry with me for saying so, my heart's all one ache. Poor people are
touchy—that's in the nature of things. I felt that even in the past. The
poor man is exacting; he takes a different view of God's world, and
looks askance at every passer-by and turns a troubled gaze about him
and looks to every word, wondering whether people are not talking
about him, whether they are saying that he is so ugly, speculating
about what he would feel exactly, what he would be on this side and
what he would be on that side, and everyone knows, Varinka, that a
poor man is worse than a rag and can get no respect from anyone;
whatever they may write, those scribblers, it will always be the same
with the poor man as it has been. And why will it always be as it has
been? Because to their thinking the poor man must be turned inside
out, he must have no privacy, no pride whatever! Emelyan told me the
other day that they got up a subscription for him and made a sort of
official inspection over every sixpence; they thought that they were
giving him his sixpences for nothing, but they were not; they were
paid for them by showing him he was a poor man. Nowadays, my dear
soul, benevolence is practised in a very queer way . . . and perhaps it
always has been so, who knows! Either people don't know how to do
it or they are first-rate hands at it—one of the two. Perhaps you did
not know it, so there it is for you. On anything else we can say nothing, but on this subject we are authorities! And how is it a poor man
knows all this and thinks of it all like this? Why?—from experience!
Because he knows for instance, that there is a gentleman at his side,
who is going somewhere to a restaurant and saying to himself,
"What's this beggarly clerk going to eat to-day? I'm going to eat *sauté
papillotte* while he is going to eat porridge without butter, maybe."
And what business is it to him that I am going to eat porridge without butter? There are men, Varinka, there are men who think of
nothing else. And they go about, the indecent caricaturists, and look
whether one puts one's whole foot down on the pavement or walks
on tiptoe; they notice that such a clerk, of such a department, a titular councillor, has his bare toes sticking out of his boot, that he has
holes in his elbow—and then they sit down at home and describe it
all and publish such rubbish . . . and what business is it of yours, sir, if

my elbows are in holes? Yes, if you will excuse me the coarse expression, Varinka, I will tell you that the poor man has the same sort of modesty on that score as you, for instance, have maidenly modesty. Why, you wouldn't divest yourself of your clothing before everyone—forgive my coarse comparison. So, in the same way, the poor man does not like people to peep into his poor hole and wonder about his domestic arrangements. So what need was there to join in insulting me, Varinka, with the enemies who are attacking an honest man's honour and reputation?

And in the office to-day I sat like a hen, like a plucked sparrow, so that I almost turned with shame at myself. I was ashamed, Varinka! And one is naturally timid, when one's elbows are seeing daylight through one's sleeves, and one's buttons are hanging on threads. And, as ill-luck would have it, all my things were in such disorder! You can't help losing heart. Why! . . . Stepan Karlovitch himself began speaking to me about my work to-day, he talked and talked away and added, as though unawares, "Well, really, Makar Alexyevitch!" and did not say what was in his mind, only I understood what it was for myself, and blushed so that even the bald patch on my head was crimson. It was really only a trifle, but still it made me uneasy, and aroused bitter reflections. If only they have heard nothing! Ah, God forbid that they should hear about anything! I confess I do suspect one man. I suspect him very much. Why, these villains stick at nothing, they will betray me, they will give away one's whole private life for a halfpenny—nothing is sacred to them.

I know now whose doing it is; it is Ratazyaev's doing. He knows someone in our office, and most likely in the course of conversation has told them the whole story with additions; or maybe he has told the story in his own office, and it has crept out and crept into our office. In our lodging, they all know it down to the lowest, and point at your window; I know that they do point. And when I went to dinner with you yesterday, they all poked their heads out of window and the landlady said: "Look," said she, "the devil has made friends with the baby." And then she called you an unseemly name. But all that's nothing beside Ratazyaev's disgusting design to put you and me into his writing and to describe us in a cunning satire; he spoke of this himself, and friendly fellow-lodgers have repeated it to me. I can think of nothing else, my darling, and don't know what to decide to do. There is no concealing the fact, we have provoked the wrath of God, little angel. You meant to send me a book, my good friend, to relieve my dullness; what is the use of a book, my love, what's the good of it? It's arrant nonsense! The story is nonsense and it is written as nonsense, just for idle people to read; trust me, my dear soul, trust the experience of my age. And what if they talk to you of some Shakespeare, saying, "You see that Shakespeare wrote literature," well, then, Shakespeare is nonsense; it's all arrant nonsense and only written to jeer at folk!

Yours,
MAKAR DYEVUSHKIN.

August 2.

DEAR MAKAR ALEXYEVITCH!

Don't worry about anything; please God it will all be set right. Fedora has got a lot of work both for herself and for me, and we have set to work very happily; perhaps we shall save the situation. She suspects that Anna Fyodorovna had some hand in this last unpleasant business; but now I don't care. I feel somehow particularly cheerful to-day. You want to borrow money—God forbid! You'll get into trouble afterwards when you need to pay it back. We had much better live more frugally; come to us more often, and don't take any notice of your landlady. As for your other enemies and ill-wishers, I am sure you are worrying yourself with needless suspicions, Makar Alexyevitch! Mind, I told you last time that your language was very exaggerated. Well, good-bye till we meet. I expect you without fail.

Your
V. D.

August 3.

MY ANGEL, VARVARA ALEXYEVNA,

I hasten to tell you, my little life, I have fresh hopes of something. But excuse me, my little daughter, you write, my angel, that I am not to borrow money. My darling, it is impossible to avoid it; here I am in a bad way, and what if anything were suddenly amiss with you! You are frail, you know; so that's why I say we must borrow. Well, so I will continue.

I beg to inform you, Varvara Alexyevna, that in the office I am sitting next to Emelyan Ivanovitch. That's not the Emelyan Ilyitch whom you know. He is, like me, a titular councillor, and he and I are almost the oldest veterans in the office. He is a good-natured soul, an unworldly soul; he's not given to talking and always sits like a regular bear. But he is a good clerk and has a good English handwriting and, to tell the whole truth, he writes as well as I do—he's a worthy man! I never was very intimate with him, but only just say good-morning and good-evening; or if I wanted the pen-knife, I would say, "Give me the pen-knife, Emelyan Ivanovitch"; in short, our intercourse was confined to our common necessities. Well so, he says to me to-day, "Makar Alexyevitch, why are you so thoughtful?" I see the man wishes me kindly, so I told him—I said, "This is how it is, Emelyan Ivanovitch"—that is, I did not tell him everything, and indeed, God forbid! I never will tell the story because I haven't the heart to, but just told him something, that I was in straits for money, and so on. "You should borrow, my good soul," said Emelyan Ivanovitch: "you should borrow; from Pyotr Petrovitch you might borrow, he lends money at interest; I have borrowed and he asks a decent rate of interest, not exorbitant." Well, Varinka, my heart gave a leap. I thought and thought maybe the Lord will put it into the heart of Pyotr Petrovitch and in his benevolence he will lend me the money. Already I was reckoning to myself that I could pay the landlady and help you, and clear myself all round. Whereas now it is such a disgrace, one is afraid to be in one's own place, let alone the jeers of our grinning jack-anapes. Bother them! And besides, his Excellency sometimes passes by our table: why, God forbid! he may cast a glance in my direction and notice I'm not decently dressed! And he makes a great point of neat-ness and tidiness. Maybe he would say nothing, but I should die of shame—that's how it would be. In consequence I screwed myself up and, putting my pride in my ragged pocket, I went up to Pyotr Petrovitch full of hope and at the same time more dead than alive with suspense. But, after all, Varinka, it all ended in foolishness! He was busy with something, talking with Fedosey Ivanovitch. I went up to him sideways and pulled him by the sleeve, saying, "Pyotr Petrovitch, I say, Pyotr Petrovitch!" He looked round, and I went on: saying, "this is how it is, thirty roubles," and so on. At first he did not understand me, and when I explained it all to him, he laughed, and said nothing. I said the same thing again. And he said to me, "Have you got a pledge?" And he buried himself in his writing and did not even glance at me. I was a little flustered. "No," I said, "Pyotr Petrovitch, I've no pledge," and I explained to him that when I got my salary I would pay him, would be sure to pay him, I should con-sider it my first duty. Then somebody called him. I waited for him, he came back and began mending a pen and did not seem to notice me, and I kept on with "Pyotr Petrovitch, can't you manage it somehow?" He said nothing and seemed not to hear me. I kept on standing there. Well, I thought I would try for the last time, and pulled him by the sleeve. He just muttered something, cleaned his pen, and began writ-ing. I walked away. You see, my dear girl, they may be excellent people, but proud, very proud—but I don't mind! We are not fit company for them, Varinka! That is why I have written all this to you. Emelyan Ivanovitch laughed, too, and shook his head, but he cheered me up, the dear fellow—Emelyan Ivanovitch is a worthy man. He promised to introduce me to a man who lives in the Vybord Side, Varinka, and lends money at interest too; he is some sort of clerk of the fourteenth class. Emelyan Ivanovitch says he will be sure to lend it. Shall I go to him to-morrow, my angel, eh? What do you think? It is awful if I don't. My landlady is almost turning me out and won't consent to give me my dinner; besides, my boots are in a dreadful state, my dear; I've no buttons either and nothing else besides. And what if anyone in authority at the office notices such unseemliness; it will be awful, Varinka, simply awful!

MAKAR DYEVUSHKIN.

August 4.

DEAR MAKAR ALEXYEVITCH,

For God's sake, Makar Alexyevitch, borrow some money as soon as possible! I would not for anything have asked you for help as things are at present, but if you only knew what a position I am in. It's utterly impossible for us to remain in this lodging. A horribly unpleasant thing has happened here, and if only you knew how upset and agitated I am! Only imagine, my friend; this morning a stranger came into our lodging, an elderly, almost old man, wearing orders. I was amazed, not knowing what he wanted with us. Fedora had gone out to a shop at the time. He began asking me how I lived and what I did, and without waiting for an answer, told me that he was the uncle of that officer; that he was very angry with his nephew for his disgraceful behaviour, and for having given us a bad name all over the buildings; said that his nephew was a featherheaded scamp, and that he was ready to take me under his protection; advised me not to listen to young men, added that he sympathised with me like a father, that he felt a father's feeling for me and was ready to help me in any way. I blushed all over, not knowing what to think, but was in no haste to thank him. He took my hand by force, patted me on the cheek, told me I was very pretty and that he was delighted to find I had dimples in my cheeks (goodness knows what he said!) and at last tried to kiss me, saying that he was an old man (he was so loathsome). At that point Fedora came in. He was a little disconcerted and began saying again that he felt respect for me, for my discretion and good principles, and that he was very anxious that I should not treat him as a stranger. Then he drew Fedora aside and on some strange pretext wanted to give her a lot of money. Fedora, of course, would not take it. At last he got up to go, he repeated once more all his assurances, said that he would come and see me again and bring me some earrings (I believe he, too, was very much embarrassed); he advised me to change my lodgings and recommended me a very nice lodging which he had his eye on, and which would cost me nothing; he said that he liked me very much for being an honest and sensible girl, advised me to beware of profligate men, and finally told us that he knew Anna Fyodorovna and that Anna Fyodorovna had commissioned him to tell me that she would come and see me herself. Then I understood it all. I don't know what came over me; it was the first time in my life I had had such an experience; I flew into a fury, I put him to shame completely. Fedora helped me, and we almost turned him out of the flat. We've come to the conclusion that it is all Anna Fyodorovna's doing; how else could he have heard of us?

Now I appeal to you, Makar Alexyevitch, and entreat you to help us. For God's sake, don't desert me in this awful position. Please borrow, get hold of some money anyway; we've no money to move with and we mustn't stay here any longer; that's Fedora's advice. We need at least thirty-five roubles; I'll pay you back the money; I'll earn it. Fedora will get me some more work in a day or two, so that if they ask a high interest, never mind it, but agree to anything. I'll pay it all back, only for God's sake, don't abandon me. I can't bear worrying you now when you are in such circumstances . . . Good-bye, Makar Alexyevitch; think of me, and God grant you are successful.

Yours,

V. D.

August 4.

My darling Varvara Alexyevna!

All these unexpected blows positively shatter me! Such terrible calamities destroy my spirit! These scoundrelly libertines and rascally old men will not only bring you, my angel, to a bed of sickness, they mean to be the death of me, too. And they will be, too, I swear they will. You know I am ready to die sooner than not help you! If I don't help you it will be the death of me, Varinka, the actual literal death of me, and if I do help you, you'll fly away from me like a bird out of its nest, to escape these owls, these birds of prey that were trying to peck her. That's what tortures me, my precious. And you too, Varinka, you are so cruel! How can you do it? You are tormented, you are insulted, you, my little bird, are in distress, and then you regret that you must worry me and promise to repay the debt, which means, to tell the truth, that with your delicate health you will kill yourself, in order to get the money for me in time. Why, only think, Varinka, what you are talking about. Why should you sew? Why should you work, worry your poor little head with anxiety, spoil your pretty eyes and destroy your health? Ah, Varinka, Varinka! You see, my darling, I am good for nothing, but I'll manage to be good for something! I will overcome all obstacles. I will get outside work, I will copy all sorts of manuscripts for all sorts of literary men. I will go to them, I won't wait to be asked, I'll force them to give me work, for you know, my darling, they are on the look-out for good copyists, I know they look out for them, but I won't let you wear yourself out; I won't let you carry out such a disastrous intention. I will certainly borrow it, my angel, I'd sooner die than not borrow it. You write, my darling, that I am not to be afraid of a high rate of interest—and I won't be afraid of it, my dear soul, I won't be frightened. I won't be frightened of anything now. I will ask for forty roubles in paper, my dear; that's not much, you know, Varinka, what do you think? Will they trust me with forty roubles at the first word? That is, I mean to say, do you consider me capable of inspiring trust and confidence at first sight. Can they form a favourable impression of me from my physiognomy at first sight? Recall my appearance, my angel; am I capable of inspiring confidence? What do you think yourself? You know I feel such terror; it makes me quite ill, to tell the truth, quite ill. Of the forty roubles I set aside twenty-five for you, Varinka, two silver roubles will be for the landlady, and the rest I design for my own expenses. You see I ought to give the landlady more, I must, in fact; but if you think it all over, my dear girl, and reckon out all I need, then you'll see that it is impossible to give her more, consequently there's no use talking about it and no need to refer to it. For a silver rouble I shall buy a pair of boots— I really don't know whether I shall be able to appear at the office in the old ones; a new necktie would have been necessary, too, for I have had the old one a year, but since you've promised to make me, not only a tie, but a shirtfront cut out of your old apron, I shall think no more of a tie. So there we have boots and a tie. Now for buttons, my dear. You will agree, my darling, that I can't go on without buttons and almost half have dropped off. I tremble when I think that his Excellency may notice such untidiness and say something, and what he would say! I shouldn't hear what he would say, my darling, for I should die, die, die on the spot, simply go and die of shame at the very thought!—Ah, Varinka!—Well, after all these necessities, there will be three roubles left, so that would do to live on and get half a pound of tobacco, for I can't live without tobacco, my little angel, and this is the ninth day since I had my pipe in my mouth. To tell the truth, I should have bought it and said nothing to you, but I was ashamed. You are there in trouble depriving yourself of everything, and here am I enjoying luxuries of all sorts; so that's why I tell you about it to escape the stings of conscience. I frankly confess, Varinka, I am now in an extremely straitened position, that is, nothing like it has ever happened before. My landlady despises me, I get no sort of respect from anyone; my terrible lapses, my debts; and at the office, where I had anything but a good time, in the old days, at the hands of my fellow clerks—now, Varinka, it is beyond words. I hide everything, I carefully hide everything from everyone, and I edge into the office sideways, I hold aloof from all. It's only to you that I have the heart to confess it. . . . And what if they won't give me the money! No, we had better not think about that, Varinka, not depress our spirits beforehand with such thoughts. That's why I am writing this, to warn you not to think about it, and not to worry yourself with evil imaginations. Ah! my God! what will happen to you then! It's true that then you will not move from that lodging and I shall be with you then. But, no, I should not come back then, I should simply perish somewhere and be lost. Here I have been writing away to you and I ought to have been shaving; it makes one more presentable, and to be presentable always counts for something. Well, God help us, I will say my prayers, and then set off.

M. DYEVUSHKIN.

August 5.

MY DEAR MAKAR ALEXYEVITCH,

You really mustn't give way to despair. There's trouble enough without that.

I send you thirty kopecks in silver, I cannot manage more. Buy yourself what you need most, so as to get along somehow, until to-morrow. We have scarcely anything left ourselves, and I don't know what will happen to-morrow. It's sad, Makar Alexyevitch! Don't be sad, though, if you've not succeeded, there's no help for it. Fedora says that there is no harm done so far, that we can stay for the time in this lodging, that if we did move we shouldn't gain much by it, and that they can find us anywhere if they want to. Though I don't feel comfortable at staying here now. If it were not so sad I would have written you an account of something.

What a strange character you have, Makar Alexyevitch; you take everything too much to heart and so you will be always a very unhappy man. I read all your letters attentively and I see in every letter you are anxious and worried about me as you never are about yourself. Everyone says, of course, that you have a good heart, but I say that it is too good. I will give you some friendly advice, Makar Alexyevitch. I am grateful to you, very grateful for all that you have done for me, I feel it very much; so judge what it must be for me to see that even now, after all your misfortunes of which I have been the unconscious cause—that even now you are only living in my life, my joys, my sorrows, my feelings! If one takes all another person's troubles so to heart and sympathises so intensely with everything it is bound to make one very unhappy. To-day, when you came in to see me from the office I was frightened at the sight of you. You were so pale, so despairing, so frightened-looking; you did not look like yourself—and all because you were afraid to tell me of your failure, afraid of disappointing me, of frightening me, and when you saw I nearly laughed your heart was almost at ease. Makar Alexyevitch, don't grieve, don't despair, be more sensible, I beg you, I implore you. Come, you will see that everything will be all right. Everything will take a better turn: why, life will be a misery to you, for ever grieving and being miserable over other people's troubles. Good-bye, my dear friend. I beseech you not to think too much about it.

V. D.

August 5.

My darling Varinka,

Very well, my angel, very well! You have made up your mind that it is no harm so far that I have not got the money. Well, very good, I feel reassured, I am happy as regards you. I am delighted, in fact, that you are not going to leave me in my old age but are going to stay in your lodging. In fact, to tell you everything, my heart was brimming over with joy when I saw that you wrote so nicely about me in your letter and gave due credit to my feelings. I don't say this from pride, but because I see how you love me when you are so anxious about my heart. Well, what's the use of talking about my heart! The heart goes its own way, but you hint, my precious, that I mustn't be down-hearted. Yes, my angel, maybe, and I say myself it is of no use being downhearted! but for all that, you tell me, my dear girl, what boots I am to go to the office in to-morrow! That's the trouble, Varinka; and you know such a thought destroys a man, destroys him utterly. And the worst of it is, my own, that it is not for myself I am troubled, it is not for myself I am distressed; as far as I am concerned I don't mind going about without an overcoat and without boots in the hardest frost; I don't care: I can stand anything, and put up with anything. I am a humble man of no importance,—but what will people say? My enemies with their spiteful tongues, what will they say, when one goes about without an overcoat ? You know it is for the sake of other people one wears an overcoat, yes, and boots, too, you put on, perhaps, on their account. Boots, in such cases, Varinka darling, are necessary to keep up one's dignity and good name: in boots with holes in them, both dignity and good name are lost; trust the experience of my years, my dear child, listen to an old man like me who knows the world and what people are, and not to any scurrilous scribblers and satirists.

I have not yet told you in detail, my darling, how it all happened to-day. I suffered so much, I endured in one morning more mental anguish than many a man endures in a year. This is how it was: first, I set off very early in the morning, so as to find him and be in time for the office afterwards. There was such a rain, such a sleet falling this morning! I wrapped myself up in my overcoat, my little dearie. I walked on and on and I kept thinking: "Oh, Lord, forgive my transgressions and grant the fulfilment of my desires!" Passing St. X's Church, I crossed myself, repented of all my sins, and thought that it was wrong of me to bargain with the Almighty. I was lost in my thoughts and did not feel like looking at anything; so I walked without picking my way. The streets were empty, and the few I met all seemed anxious and preoccupied, and no wonder: who would go out at such an early hour and in such weather! A gang of workmen, grinning all over, met me, the rough fellows shoved against me! A feeling of dread came over me, I felt panic-stricken, to tell the truth I didn't like even to think about the money— I felt I must just take my chance! Just at Voskressensky Bridge the sole came off my boot, so I really don't know what I walked upon. And then I met our office attendant, Yermolaev. He drew himself up at attention and stood looking after me as though he would ask for a drink. "Ech, a drink, brother," I thought; "not much chance of a drink!" I was awfully tired. I stood still, rested a bit and pushed on farther; I looked about on purpose for something to fasten my attention on, to distract my mind, to cheer me up, but no, I couldn't fix one thought on anything and, besides, I was so muddy that I felt ashamed of myself. At last I saw in the distance a yellow wooden house with an upper storey in the style of a belvedere. "Well," thought I, "so that's it, that's how Emelyan Ivanovitch described it—Markov's house." (It is this Markov himself, Varinka, who lends money.) I scarcely knew what I was doing, and I knew, of course, that it was Markov's house, but I asked a police-man. "Whose house is that, brother?" said I. The policeman was a surly fellow, seemed loth to speak and cross with someone; he filtered his words through his teeth, but he did say it was Markov's house. These policemen are always so unfeeling, but what did the policeman mat-ter?—well, it all made a bad and unpleasant impression, in short, there was one thing on the top of another; one finds in everything something akin to one's own position, and it is always so. I took three turns past the house, along the street, and the further I went, the worse I felt. "No," I thought, "he won't give it me, nothing will induce him to give it me. I am a stranger and it's a ticklish business, and I am not an attractive figure. Well," I thought, "leave it to Fate, if only I do not regret it afterwards; they won't devour me for making the attempt," and I softly opened the gate, and then another misfortune happened. A wretched, stupid yard dog fastened upon me. It was beside itself and barked its loudest!—and it's just such wretched, trivial incidents that always madden a man, Varinka, and make him nervous and destroy all the determination he has been fortifying himself with beforehand; so that I went into the house more dead than alive and walked straight into trouble again. Without seeing what was below me straight in the doorway, I went in, stumbled over a woman who was busy straining some milk from a pail into a jug, and spilt all the milk. The silly woman shrieked and made an outcry, saying, "Where are you shoving to, my man?" and made a deuce of a row. I may say, Varinka, it is always like this with me in such cases; it seems it is my fate, I always get mixed up in something. An old hag, the Finnish landlady, poked her head out at the noise. I went straight up to her. "Does Markov live here?" said I. "No," said she. She stood still and took a good look at me. "And what do you want with him?" I explained to her that Emelyan had told me this and that, and all the rest of it—said it was a matter of business. The old woman called her daughter, a barelegged girl in her teens. "Call your father; he's upstairs at the lodger's, most likely."

I went in. The room was all right, there were pictures on the wall—all portraits of generals, a sofa, round table, mignonette, and balsam—I wondered whether I had not better clear out and take myself off for good and all. And, oh dear, I did want to run away, Varinka. "I had better come to-morrow," I thought, "and the weather will be better and I will wait a little—to-day the milk's been spilt and the generals look so cross . . ." I was already at the door—but he came in—a grey-headed man with thievish eyes, in a greasy dressing-gown with a cord round his waist. He enquired how and why, and I told him that Emelyan Ivanovitch had told me this and that—"Forty roubles," I said, "is what I've come about"—and I couldn't finish. I saw from his eyes that the game was lost. "No," says he; "the fact is, I've no money; and have you brought anything to pledge as security?"

I began explaining that I had brought nothing to pledge, but that Emelyan Ivanovitch—I explained in fact, what was wanted. He heard it all. "No," said he; "what is Emelyan Ivanovitch! I've no money."

Well, I thought, "There it is, I knew—I had a foreboding of it."

Well, Varinka, it would have been better really if the earth had opened under me. I felt chill all over, my feet went numb and a shiver ran down my back. I looked at him and he looked at me and almost said, Come, run along, brother, it is no use your staying here—so that if such a thing had happened in other circumstances, I should have been quite ashamed. "And what do you want money for?"—(do you know, he asked that, Varinka). I opened my mouth, if only not to stand there doing nothing, but he wouldn't listen. "No," he said, "I have no money, I would have lent it with pleasure," said he. Then I pressed him, telling him I only wanted a little, saying I would pay him back on the day fixed, that I would pay him back before the day fixed, that he could ask any interest he liked and that, by God! I would pay him back. At that instant, my darling, I thought of you, I thought of all your troubles and privations, I thought of your poor little half-rouble. "But no," says he, "the interest is no matter; if there had been a pledge now! Besides, I have no money. I have none, by God! or I'd oblige you with pleasure,"—he took God's name, too, the villain!

Well, I don't remember, my own, how I went out, how I walked along Vyborgsky Street; how I got to Voskressensky Bridge. I was fearfully tired, shivering, wet through, and only succeeded in reaching the office at ten o'clock. I wanted to brush the mud off, but Snyegirev, the porter, said I mustn't, I should spoil the brush, and "the brush is government property," said he. That's how they all go on now, my dear, these gentry treat me no better than a rag to wipe their boots on. Do you know what is killing me, Varinka? it's not the money that's killing me, but all these little daily cares, these whispers, smiles and jokes. His Excellency may by chance have to refer to me. Oh, my darling, my golden days are over. I read over all your letters to-day; it's sad, Varinka! Good-bye, my own! The Lord keep you.

M. DYEVUSHKIN.

P.S.—I meant to describe my troubles half in joke, Varinka, only it seems that it does not come off with me, joking. I wanted to satisfy you. I am coming to see you, my dear girl, I will be sure to come.

August 11.

VARVARA ALEXYEVNA, MY DARLING,

I am lost, we are both lost, both together irretrievably lost. My reputation, my dignity—all is destroyed! I am ruined and you are ruined, my darling. You are hopelessly ruined with me! It's my doing, I have brought you to ruin! I am persecuted, Varinka, I am despised, turned into a laughing-stock, and the landlady has simply begun to abuse me; she shouted and shouted at me, to-day; she rated and rated at me and treated me as though I were dirt. And in the evening, at Ratazyaev's, one of them began reading aloud the rough copy of a letter to you which I had accidentally dropped out of my pocket. My precious, what a joke they made of it! They called us all sorts of flattering names and roared with laughter, the traitors! I went to them and taxed Ratazyaev with his perfidy, told him he was a traitor! And Ratazyaev answered that I was a traitor myself, that I amused myself with making conquests among the fair sex. He said, "You take good care to keep it from us; you're a Lovelace," he said; and now they all call me Lovelace and I have no other name! Do you hear, my little angel, do you hear?—they know it all now, they know all about it, and they know about you, my own, and whatever you have, they know about it all! And that's not all. Even Faldoni is in it, he's following their lead; I sent him to-day to the sausage-shop to get me something; he wouldn't go. "I am busy," that was all he said! "But you know it's your duty," I said. "No, indeed," he said, "it's not my duty. Here, you don't pay my mistress her money, so I have no duty to you." I could not stand this insult from him, an illiterate peasant, and I said, "You fool," and he answered back, "Fool yourself." I thought he must have had a drop too much to be so rude, and I said: "You are drunk, you peasant!" and he answered: "Well, not at your expense, anyway, you've nothing to get drunk on yourself; you are begging for twenty kopecks from somebody yourself," and he even added: "Ugh! and a gentleman too!" There, my dear girl, that's what it has come to! One's ashamed to be alive, Varinka! As though one were some sort of outcast, worse than a tramp without a passport. An awful calamity! I am ruined, simply ruined! I am irretrievably ruined!

M. D.

August 13.

MY DEAR MAKAR ALEXYEVITCH,

It's nothing but one trouble after another upon us. I don't know myself what to do! What will happen to you now?—and I have very little to hope for either; I burnt my left hand this morning with an iron; I dropped it accidentally and bruised myself and burnt my hand at the same time. I can't work at all, and Fedora has been poorly for the last three days. I am in painful anxiety. I send you thirty kopecks in silver; it is almost all we have left, and God knows how I should have liked to help you in your need. I am so vexed I could cry. Good-bye, my friend! You would comfort me very much if you would come and see us to-day.

V. D.

August 14.

MAKAR ALEXYEVITCH

What is the matter with you? It seems you have no fear of God! You are simply driving me out of my mind. Aren't you ashamed? You will be your own ruin; you should at least think of your good name! You're a man of honour, of gentlemanly feelings, of self-respect; well, when everyone finds out about you! Why, you will simply die of shame! Have you no pity for your grey hairs? Have you no fear of God? Fedora says she won't help you again, and I won't give you money either. What have you brought me to, Makar Alexyevitch? I suppose you think that it is nothing to me, your behaving so badly? You don't know what I have to put up with on your account! I can't even go down our staircase; everyone looks at me and points at me, and says such awful things; they say plainly that I have *taken up with a drunkard.* Think what it is to hear that! When you are brought in all the lodgers point at you with contempt: "Look," they say, "they've brought that clerk in." And I'm ready to faint with shame over you. I swear I shall move from here. I shall go somewhere as a housemaid or a laundrymaid, I shan't stay here. I wrote to you to come and see me here but you did not come. So are my tears and entreaties nothing to you, Makar Alexyevitch? And where do you get the money? For God's sake, do be careful. Why, you are ruining yourself, ruining yourself for nothing! And it's a shame and a disgrace! The landlady would not let you in last night, you spent the night in the porch. I know all about it. If only you knew how miserable I was when I knew all about it. Come to see me; you will be happy with us; we will read together, we will recall the past. Fedora will tell us about her wanderings as a pilgrim. For my sake, don't destroy yourself and me. Why, I only live for you, for your sake I am staying with you. And this is how you are behaving now! Be a fine man, steadfast in misfortune, remember that poverty is not a vice. And why despair? It is all temporary! Please God, it will all be set right, only you must restrain yourself now. I sent you twenty kopecks. Buy yourself tobacco or anything you want, only for God's sake don't spend it on what's harmful. Come and see us, be sure to come. Perhaps you will be ashamed as you were before, but don't be ashamed; it's false shame. If only you would show genuine penitence. Trust in God. He will do all things for the best.

V. D.

August 19.

VARVARA ALEXYEVNA, DARLING,

I am ashamed, little dearie, Varvara Alexyevna; I am quite ashamed. But, after all, what is there so particular about it, my dear? Why not rejoice the heart a little? Then I don't think about my sole, for one's sole is nonsense, and will always remain a simple, nasty, muddy sole. Yes, and boots are nonsense, too! The Greek sages used to go about without boots, so why should people like us pamper ourselves with such unworthy objects? Oh! my dearie, my dearie, you have found something to write about! You tell Fedora that she is a nonsensical, fidgety, fussy woman, and, what's more, she's a silly one, too, unutterably silly! As for my grey hairs, you are quite mistaken about that, my own, for I am by no means so old as you think. Emelyan sends you his regards. You write that you have been breaking your heart and crying; and I write to you that I am breaking my heart, too, and crying. In conclusion I wish you the best of health and prosperity, and as for me I am in the best of health and prosperity, too, and I remain, my angel, your friend,

MAKAR DYEVUSHKIN.

August 21.

HONOURED MADAM AND DEAR FRIEND, VARVARA ALEXYEVNA,

I feel that I am to blame, I feel that I have wronged you, and to my mind there's no benefit at all, dear friend, in my feeling it, whatever you may say. I felt all that even before my misconduct, but I lost heart and fell, knowing I was doing wrong. My dear, I am not a bad man and not cruel-hearted, and to torture your little heart, my little darling, one must be, more or less, like a bloodthirsty tiger. Well, I have the heart of a lamb and, as you know, have no inclination towards bloodthirstiness; consequently, my angel, I am not altogether to blame in my misconduct, since neither my feelings nor my thoughts were to blame; and in fact, I don't know what was to blame; it's all so incomprehensible, my darling! you sent me thirty kopecks in silver, and then you sent me twenty kopecks. My heart ached looking at your poor little coins. You had burnt your hand, you would soon be going hungry yourself, and you write that I am to buy tobacco. Well, how could I behave in such a position? Was I without a pang of conscience to begin plundering you, poor little orphan, like a robber! Then I lost heart altogether, my darling—that is, at first I could not help feeling that I was good for nothing and that I was hardly better than the sole of my boot. And so I felt it was unseemly to consider myself of any consequence, and began to look upon myself as something unseemly and somewhat indecent. Well, and when I lost my self-respect and denied my good qualities and my dignity, then it was all up with me, it meant degradation, inevitable degradation! That is ordained by destiny and I'm not to blame for it.

I went out at first to get a little air, then it was one thing after another; nature was so tearful, the weather was cold and it was raining. Well, Emelyan turned up. He had pawned everything he had, Varinka, everything he had is gone: and when I met him he had not put a drop of the rosy to his lips for two whole days and nights, so that he was ready to pawn what you can't pawn, because such things are never taken in pawn. Well, Varinka, I gave way more from a feeling of humanity than my own inclination, that's how the sin came to pass, my dear! How we wept together! We spoke of you. He's very good-natured, he's a very good-natured fellow and a very feeling man. I feel all that myself, my dear girl, that is just why it all happens to me, that I feel it all very much. I know how much I owe to you, my darling. Getting to know you, I came first to know myself better and to love you; and before I knew you, my angel, I was solitary and as it were asleep, and scarcely alive. They said, the spiteful creatures, that even my appearance was unseemly and they were disgusted with me, and so I began to be disgusted with myself; they said I was stupid and I really thought that I was stupid. When you came to me, you lighted up my dark life, so that my heart and my soul were filled with light and I gained peace at heart, and knew that I was no worse than others; that the only thing is that I am not brilliant in any way, that I have no polish or style about me, but I am still a man, in heart and mind a man. Well now, feeling that I was persecuted and humiliated by destiny, I lost all faith in my own good qualities, and, shattered by calamities, I lost all heart. And now since you know all about it, my dear, I beg you with tears not to question me further about that matter, for my heart is breaking and it is very bitter for me and hard to bear.

Assuring you of my respect, I remain, your faithful

MAKAR DYEVUSHKIN.

September 3.

I did not finish my last letter, Makar Alexyevitch, because it was difficult for me to write. Sometimes I have moments when I am glad to be alone, to mourn, with none to share my grief, and such moments are becoming more and more frequent with me. In my recollections there is something inexplicable to me, which attacks me unaccountably and so intensely that for hours at a stretch I am insensible to all surrounding me and I forget everything—all the present. And there is no impression of my present life, whether pleasant or painful and sad, which would not remind me of something similar in my past, and most often in my childhood, my golden childhood! But I always feel oppressed after such moments. I am somehow weakened by them; my dreaminess exhausts me, and apart from that my health grows worse and worse. But to-day the fresh bright sunny morning, such as are rare in autumn here, revived me and I welcomed it joyfully. And so autumn is with us already! How I used to love the autumn in the country! I was a child then, but I had already felt a great deal. I loved the autumn evening better than the morning. I remember that there was a lake at the bottom of the hill a few yards from our house. That lake—I feel as though I could see it now—that lake was so broad, so smooth, as bright and clear as crystal! At times, if it were a still evening, the lake was calm; not a leaf would stir on the trees that grew on the bank, and the water would be as motionless as a mirror. It was so fresh, so cool! The dew would be falling on the grass, the lights begin twinkling in the cottages on the bank, and they would be driving the cattle home. Then I could creep out to look at my lake, and I would forget everything, looking at it. At the water's edge, the fishermen would have a faggot burning and the light would be reflected far, far, over the water. The sky was so cold and blue, with streaks of fiery red along the horizon, and the streaks kept growing paler and paler; the moon would rise; the air so resonant that if a frightened bird fluttered, or a reed stirred in the faint breeze, or a fish splashed in the water, everything could be heard. A white steam, thin and transparent, rises up over the blue water: the distance darkens; everything seems drowned in the mist, while close by it all stands out so sharply, as though cut by a chisel, the boat, the banks, the islands; the tub thrown away and forgotten floats in the water close to the bank, the willow branch hangs with its yellow leaves tangled in the reeds, a belated gull flies up, then dives into the cold water, flies up again and is lost in the mist—while I gaze and listen. How lovely, how marvellous it was to me! and I was a child, almost a baby. . . .

I was so fond of the autumn, the late autumn when they were carrying the harvest, finishing all the labours of the year, when the peasants began gathering together in their cottages in the evening, when they were all expecting winter. Then it kept growing darker. The yellow leaves strewed the paths at the edges of the bare forest while the forest grew bluer and darker—especially at evening when a damp mist fell and the trees glimmered in the mist like giants, like terrible misshapen phantoms. If one were late out for a walk, dropped behind the others, how one hurried on alone—it was dreadful! One trembled like a leaf and kept thinking that in another minute someone terrible would peep out from behind that hollow tree; meanwhile the wind would rush through the woods, roaring and whistling, howling so plaintively, tearing a crowd of leaves from a withered twig, whirling them in the air, and with wild, shrill cries the birds would fly after them in a great, noisy flock, so that the sky would be all covered and darkened with them. One feels frightened, and then, just as though one heard someone speaking—some voice—as though someone whispered: "Run, run, child, don't be late; it will be dreadful here soon; run, child!"—with a thrill of horror at one's heart one would run till one was out of breath. One would reach home, breathless; there it was all noise and gaiety; all of us children had some work given to us to do, shelling peas or shaking out poppy seeds. The damp wood crackles in the stove. Cheerfully mother looks after our cheerful work; our old nurse, Ulyana, tells us stories about old times or terrible tales of wizards and dead bodies. We children squeeze up to one another with smiles on our lips. Then suddenly we are all silent . . . Oh! a noise as though someone were knocking—it was nothing; it was old Frolovna's spindle; how we laughed! Then at night we would lie awake for hours, we had such fearful dreams. One would wake and not dare to stir, and lie shivering under the quilt till daybreak. In the morning one would get up, fresh as a flower. One would look out of the window; all the country would be covered with frost, the thin hoarfrost of autumn would be hanging on the bare boughs, the lake would be covered with ice, thin as a leaf, a white mist would be rising over it, the birds would be calling merrily, the sun would light up everything with its brilliant rays and break the thin ice like glass. It was so bright, so shining, so gay, the fire would be crackling in the stove again, we would sit down round the samovar while our black dog, Polkan, numb with cold from the night, would peep in at the window with a friendly wag of his tail. A peasant would ride by the window on his good horse to fetch wood from the forest. Everyone was so gay, so happy! . . . There were masses and masses of corn stored up in the threshing-barns; the huge, huge stacks covered with straw shone golden in the sun, a comforting sight! And all are calm and joyful. God has blessed us all with the harvest; they all know they will have bread for the winter; the peasant knows that his wife and children will have food to eat; and so there is no end to the singing of the girls and their dances and games in the evening, and on the Saints' days! All pray in the house of God with grateful tears! Oh! what a golden, golden age was my childhood! . . .

Here I am crying like a child, carried away by my reminiscences. I remembered it all so vividly, so vividly, all the past stood out so brightly before me, and the present is so dim, so dark! . . . How will it end, how will it all end? Do you know I have a sort of conviction, a feeling of certainty, that I shall die this autumn. I am very, very ill. I often think about dying, but still I don't want to die like this, to lie in the earth here. Perhaps I shall be laid up as I was in the spring; I've not fully recovered from that illness yet. I am feeling very dreary just now.

Fedora has gone off somewhere for the whole day and I am sitting alone. And for some time now I've been afraid of being left alone; I always feel as though there were someone else in the room, that someone is talking to me; especially when I begin dreaming about something and suddenly wake up from my brooding, then I feel frightened. That is why I've written you such a long letter; it goes off when I write. Good-bye; I finish my letter because I have neither time nor paper for more. Of the money from pawning my dress and my hat I have only one rouble in silver left. You have given the landlady two roubles in silver; that's very good. She will keep quiet now for a time.

You must improve your clothes somehow. Good-bye, I'm so tired; I don't know why I am growing so feeble. The least work exhausts me. If I do get work, how am I to work? It is that thought that's killing me.

V. D.

September 5.

MY DARLING VARINKA,

I have received a great number of impressions this morning, my angel. To begin with I had a headache all day. To freshen myself up a bit I went for a walk along Fontanka. It was such a damp, dark evening. By six o'clock it was getting dusk—that is what we are coming to now. It was not raining but there was mist equal to a good rain. There were broad, long stretches of storm-cloud across the sky. There were masses of people walking along the canal bank, and, as ill-luck would have it, the people had such horrible depressing faces, drunken peasants, snub-nosed Finnish women, in high boots with nothing on their heads, workmen, cab-drivers, people like me out on some errand, boys, a carpenter's apprentice in a striped dressing-gown, thin and wasted-looking, with his face bathed in smutty oil, and a lock in his hand; a discharged soldier seven feet high waiting for somebody to buy a pen-knife or a bronze ring from him. That was the sort of crowd. It seems it was an hour when no other sort of people could be about. Fontanka is a canal for traffic! Such a mass of barges that one wonders how there can be room for them all! On the bridges there are women sitting with wet gingerbread and rotten apples, and they all of them looked so muddy, so drenched. It's dreary walking along Fontanka! The wet granite under one's feet, with tall, black, sooty houses on both sides. Fog underfoot and fog overhead. How dark and melancholy it was this evening!

When I went back to Gorohovoy Street it was already getting dark and they had begun lighting the gas. I have not been in Gorohovoy

Street for quite a long while, I haven't happened to go there. It's a noisy street! What shops, what magnificent establishments; everything is simply shining and resplendent; materials, flowers under glass, hats of all sorts with ribbons. One would fancy they were all displayed as a show—but no: you know there are people who buy all those things and present them to their wives. It's a wealthy street! There are a great many German bakers in Gorohovoy Street, so they must be a very prosperous set of people, too. What numbers of carriages roll by every minute; I wonder the paving is not worn out! Such gorgeous equipages, windows shining like mirrors, silk and velvet inside, and aristocratic footmen wearing epaulettes and carrying a sword; I glanced into all the carriages, there were always ladies in them dressed up to the nines, perhaps countesses and princesses. No doubt it was the hour when they were all hastening to balls and assemblies. It would be interesting to get a closer view of princesses and ladies of rank in general; it must be very nice; I have never seen them; except just as to-day, a passing glance at their carriages. I thought of you then. Ah, my darling, my own! When I think of you my heart begins aching! Why are you so unlucky, my Varinka? You are every bit as good as any of them. You are good, lovely, well-educated—why has such a cruel fortune fallen to your lot? Why does it happen that a good man is left forlorn and forsaken, while happiness seems thrust upon another? I know, I know, my dear, that it's wrong to think that, that it is free-thinking; but to speak honestly, to speak the whole truth, why is it fate, like a raven, croaks good fortune for one still unborn, while another begins life in the orphan asylum? And you know it often happens that Ivan the fool is favoured by fortune. "You, Ivan the fool, rummage in the family money bags, eat, drink nd be merry, while you, So-and-so, can lick your lips. That's all you are fit for, you, brother So-and-so!" It's a sin, my darling, it's a sin to think like that, but sometimes one cannot help sin creeping into one's heart. You ought to be driving in such a carriage, my own little dearie. Generals should be craving the favour of a glance from you—not the likes of us; you ought to be dressed in silk and gold, instead of a little old linen gown. You would not be a thin, delicate little thing, as you are now, but like a little sugar figure, fresh, plump and rosy. And then, I should be happy simply to look in at you from the street through the brightly lighted windows; simply to see your shadow. The thought that you were happy and gay, my pretty little bird, would be enough to make me gay, too. But as it is, it is not enough that spiteful people have ruined you, a worthless profligate wretch goes and insults you. Because his coat hangs smartly on him, because he stares at you from a golden eyeglass, the shameless fellow, he can do what he likes, and one must listen to what he says indulgently, however unseemly it is! Wait a bit—is it really so, my pretty gentlemen? And why is all this? Because you are an orphan, because you are defencelsss, because you have no powerful friend to help and protect you. And what can one call people who are ready to insult an orphan? They are worthless beasts, not men; simply trash. They are mere ciphers and have no real existence, of that I am convinced. That's what they are like, these people! And to my thinking, my own, the hurdy-gurdy man I met to-day in Gorohovoy Street is more worthy of respect than they are. He goes about the whole day long, hoping to get some wretched spare farthing for food, but he is his own master, he does earn his own living. He won't ask for charity; but he works like a machine wound up to give pleasure. "Here," he says, "I do what I can to give pleasure." He's a beggar, he's a beggar, it is true, he's a beggar all the same, but he's an honourable beggar; he is cold and weary, but still he works; though it's in his own way, still he works. And there are many honest men, my darling, who, though they earn very little in proportion to the amount and usefulness of their work, yet they bow down to no one and buy their bread of no one. Here I am just like that hurdy-gurdy man—that is, not at all like him. But in my own sense, in an honourable and aris-tocratic sense, just as he does, to the best of my abilities, I work as I can. That's enough about me, it's neither here nor there.

I speak of that hurdy-gurdy, my darling, because it has happened that I have felt my poverty twice as much to-day. I stopped to look at the hurdy-gurdy man. I was in such a mood that I stopped to distract my thoughts. I was standing there, and also two cab-drivers, a woman of some sort, and a little girl, such a grubby little thing. The hurdy-gurdy man stopped before the windows of a house. I noticed a little boy about ten years old; he would have been pretty, but he looked so ill, so frail, with hardly anything but his shirt on and almost barefoot, with his mouth open; he was listening to the music—like a child! He watched the German's dolls dancing, while his own hands and feet were numb with cold; he shivered and nibbled the edge of his sleeve. I noticed that he had a bit of paper of some sort in his hands. A gen-tleman passed and flung the hurdy-gurdy man some small coin, which fell straight into the box in a little garden in which the toy Frenchman was dancing with the ladies. At the clink of the coin the boy started, looked round and evidently thought that I had given the money. He ran up to me, his little hands trembling, his little voice trembling, he held the paper out to me and said, "A letter." I opened the letter; well, it was the usual thing, saying: "Kind gentleman, a mother's dying with three children hungry, so help us now, and as I am dying I will pray for you, my benefactor, in the next world for not forgetting my babes now." Well, what of it?—one could see what it meant, an everyday matter, but what could I give him? Well, I gave him nothing, and how sorry I was! The boy was poor, blue with cold, perhaps hungry, too, and not lying, surely he was not lying, I know that for certain. But what is wrong is that these horrid mothers don't take care of their children and send them out half naked in the cold to beg. Maybe she's a weak-willed, silly woman; and there's no one, maybe, to do anything for her, so she simply sits with her legs tucked under her, maybe she's really ill. Well, anyway, she should apply in the proper quarter. Though, maybe, she's a cheat and sends a hungry, delicate child out on purpose to deceive people, and makes him ill. And what sort of training is it for a poor boy? It simply hardens his heart, he runs about begging, people pass and have no time for him. Their hearts are stony, their words are cruel. "Get away, go along, you are naughty!" that is what he hears from everyone, and the child's heart grows hard, and in vain the poor little frightened boy shivers with cold like a fledgling fallen out of a broken nest. His hands and feet are frozen, he gasps for breath. The next thing he is coughing, before long disease, like an unclean reptile, creeps into his bosom and death is standing over him in some dark corner, no help, no escape, and that's his life! That is what life is like sometimes! Oh, Varinka, it's wretched to hear "for Christ's sake," and to pass by and give nothing, telling him "God will provide." Sometimes "for Christ's sake" is all right (it's not always the same, you know, Varinka), sometimes it's a long, drawling, habitual, practised, regular beggar's whine; it's not so painful to refuse one like that; he's an old hand, a beggar by profession. He's accustomed to it, one thinks; he can cope with it and knows how to cope with it. Sometimes "for Christ's sake" sounds unaccustomed, rude, terrible— as to-day, when I was taking the letter from the boy, a man standing close to the fence, not begging from everyone, said to me: "Give us a halfpenny, sir, for Christ's sake," and in such a harsh, jerky voice that I started with a horrible feeling and did not give him a halfpenny, I hadn't one. Rich people don't like the poor to complain aloud of their harsh lot, they say they disturb them, they are troublesome! Yes, indeed, poverty is always troublesome; maybe their hungry groans hinder the rich from sleeping!

To make a confession, my own, I began to describe all this to you partly to relieve my heart but chiefly to give you an example of the fine style of my composition, for you have no doubt noticed yourself, my dear girl, that of late my style has been forming, but such a depression came over me that I began to pity my feelings to the depth of my soul, and though I know, my dear, that one gets no good by self-pity, yet one must do oneself justice in some way, and often, my own, for no reason whatever, one literally annihilates oneself, makes oneself of no account, and not worth a straw. And perhaps that is why it happens that I am panic-stricken and persecuted like that poor boy who asked me for alms. Now I will tell you, by way of instance and illustration, Varinka; listen: hurrying to the office early in the morning, my own, I sometimes look at the town, how it wakes, gets up, begins smoking, hurrying with life, resounding—sometimes you feel so small before such a sight that it is as though someone had given you a flip on your intrusive nose and you creep along your way noiseless as water, and humble as grass, and hold your peace! Now just look into it and see what is going on in those great, black smutty buildings. Get to the bottom of that and then judge whether one was right to abuse oneself for no reason and to be reduced to undignified mortification. Note, Varinka, that I am speaking figuratively, not in a literal sense. But let us look what is going on in those houses. There, in some smoky corner, in some damp hole, which, through poverty, passes as a lodging, some workman wakes up from his sleep; and all night he has been dreaming of boots, for instance, which he had accidentally slit the day before, as though a man ought to dream of such nonsense! But he's an artisan, he's a shoemaker; it's excusable for him to think of nothing but his own subject. His children are crying and his wife is hungry; and it's not only shoemakers who get up in the morning like that, my own—that would not matter, and would not be worth writing about, but this is the point, Varinka: close by in the same house, in a storey higher or lower, a wealthy man in his gilded apartments dreams at night, it may be, of those same boots, that is, boots in a different manner, in a different sense, but still boots, for in the sense I am using the word, Varinka, everyone of us is a bit of a shoemaker, my darling; and that would not matter, only it's a pity there is no one at that wealthy person's side, no man who could whisper in his ear: "Come, give over thinking of such things, thinking of nothing but yourself, living for nothing but yourself; your children are healthy, your wife is not begging for food. Look about you, can't you see some object more noble to worry about than your boots?" That's what I wanted to say to you in a figurative way, Varinka. Perhaps it's too free a thought, my own, but sometimes one has that thought, sometimes it comes to one and one cannot help its bursting out from one's heart in warm language. And so it seems there was no reason to make oneself so cheap, and to be scared by mere noise and uproar. I will conclude by saying, Varinka, that perhaps you think what I am saying is unjust, or that I'm suffering from a fit of the spleen, or that I have copied this out of some book. No, my dear girl, you must dismiss that idea, it is not that; I abominate injustice, I am not suffering from spleen, and I've not copied anything out of a book—so there.

I went home in a melancholy frame of mind; I sat down to the table and heated my teapot to have a glass or two of tea. Suddenly I saw coming towards me Gorshkov, our poor lodger. I had noticed in the morning that he kept hanging about round the other lodgers, and trying to approach me. And I may say, in passing, Varinka, that they live ever so much worse than I do. Yes, indeed, he has a wife and children! So that if I were in his place I don't know what I should do. Well, my Gorshkov comes up to me, bows to me, a running tear as always on his eyelashes, he scrapes with his foot and can't utter a word. I made him sit down on a chair—it was a broken one, it is true, but there was no other. I offered him some tea. He refused from politeness, refused for a long time, but at last he took a glass. He would have drunk it without sugar, began apologising again, when I tried to persuade him that he must have sugar; he argued for a long time, kept refusing, but at last put the very smallest lump of sugar in his glass, and began declaring that his tea was extremely sweet. Oh, to what degradation poverty does reduce people! "Well, my good friend, what is it?" I said. "Well, it is like this, Makar Alexyevitch, my benefactor," he said, "show the mercy of the Lord, come to the help of my unhappy family; my wife and children have nothing to eat; think what it is for me, their father," said he. I tried to speak, but he interrupted me. "I am afraid of everyone here, Makar Alexyevitch—that is, not exactly afraid but as it were ashamed with them; they are all proud and haughty people. I would not have troubled you, my benefactor, I know that you have been in difficulties yourself, I know you can't give me much, but do lend me a trifle, and I make bold to ask you," said he, "because I know your kind heart. I know that you are in need yourself, that you know what trouble is now, and so your heart feels compassion." He ended by saying, "Forgive my boldness and unmannerliness, Makar Alexyevitch." I answered him that I should be heartily glad, but that I had nothing, absolutely nothing. "Makar Alexyevitch, sir," said he, "I am not asking for much, but you see it is like this—(then he flushed crimson)—my wife, my children, hungry—if only a ten-kopeck piece." Well, it sent a twinge to my heart. Why, I thought, they are worse off than I, even. Twenty kopecks was all I had left, and I was reckoning on it. I meant to spend it next day on my most pressing needs.

"No, my dear fellow, I can't, it is like this," I said.

"Makar Alexyevitch, my dear soul, what you like," he said, "if it is only ten kopecks."

Well, I took my twenty kopecks out of my box, Varinka, and gave it him; it's a good deed anyway! Ah! poverty! I had a good talk with him: "Why, how is it, my good soul," I said, "that you are in such want and yet you rent a room for five silver roubles?" He explained to me that he had taken it six months before and paid for it six months in advance; and since then circumstances had been such that the poor fellow does not know which way to turn. He expected his case would be over by this time. It's an unpleasant business. You see, Varinka, he has to answer for something before the court, he is mixed up in a case with a merchant who swindled the government over a contract; the cheat was discovered and the merchant was arrested and he's managed to implicate Gorshkov, who had something to do with it, too. But in reality Gorshkov was only guilty of negligence, of injudiciousness and unpardonable disregard of the interests of government. The case has been going on for some years. Gorshkov has had to face all sorts of difficulties.

"I'm not guilty, not in the least guilty of the dishonesty attributed to me," said Gorshkov; "I am not guilty of swindling and robbery."

This case has thrown a slur on his character; he has been turned out of the service, and though he has not been found guilty of any legal crime, yet, till he has completely cleared himself he cannot recover from the merchant a considerable sum of money due to him which is now the subject of dispute before the courts. I believe him, but the court won't take his word for it; the case is all in such a coil and a tangle that it would take a hundred years to unravel it. As soon as they untie one knot the merchant brings forward another and then another. I feel the deepest sympathy for Gorshkov, my own, I am very sorry for him. The man's out of work, he won't be taken anywhere without a character; all they had saved has been spent on food, the case is complicated and, meanwhile, they have had to live, and meanwhile, apropos of nothing and most inappropriately, a baby has been born, and that is an expense; his son fell ill—expense; died—expense; his wife is ill; he's afflicted with some disease of long standing—in fact, he has suffered, he has suffered to the utmost; he says, however, that he is expecting a favourable conclusion to his business in a day or two and that there is no doubt of it now. I am sorry for him, I am sorry for him; I am very sorry for him, Varinka. I was kind to him, he's a poor lost, scared creature; he needs a friend so I was kind to him. Well, good-bye, my dear one, Christ be with you, keep well. My darling! when I think of you it's like laying a salve on my sore heart. And though I suffer for you, yet it eases my heart to suffer for you.

Your true friend,
Makar Dyevushkin.

September 9.

My Darling, Varvara Alexyevna,

I am writing to you almost beside myself. I have been thoroughly upset by a terrible incident. My head is going round. Ah, my own, what a thing I have to tell you now! This we did not foresee. No, I don't believe that I did not foresee it; I did foresee it all. I had a presentiment of it in my heart. I even dreamed of something of the kind a day or two ago.

This is what happened! I will write to you regardless of style, just as God puts it into my heart. I went to the office to-day. I went in, I sat down, I began writing. And you must know, Varinka, that I was writing yesterday too. Well, this is how it was: Timofey Ivanovitch came up to me and was pleased to explain to me in person, "The document is wanted in a hurry," said he. "Copy it very clearly as quickly as possible and carefully, Makar Alexyevitch," he said; "it goes to be signed to-day." I must observe, my angel, that I was not myself yesterday, I could not bear the sight of anything; such a mood of sadness and depression had come over me! It was cold in my heart and dark in my soul, you were in my mind all the while, my little dearie. But I set to work to copy it; I copied it clearly, legibly, only—I really don't know how to explain it—whether the devil himself muddled me, or whether it was ordained by some secret decree of destiny, or simply it had to be—but I left out a whole line, goodness knows what sense it made, it simply made none at all. They were late with the document yesterday and only took it to his Excellency to be signed to-day. I turned up this morning at the usual hour as though nothing had happened and settled myself beside Emelyan Ivanovitch. I must observe, my own, that of late I have been more abashed and ill at ease than ever. Of late I have given up looking at anyone. If I hear so much as a chair creak I feel more dead than alive. That is just how it was to-day, I sat down like a hedgehog crouched up and shrinking into myself, so that Efim Akimovitch (there never was such a fellow for teasing) said in the hearing of all: "Why are you sitting like a picture of misery, Makar Alexyevitch?" And he made such a grimace that everyone sitting near him and me went off into roars of laughter, and at my expense of course. And they went on and on. I put my hands over my ears, and screwed up my eyes, I sat without stirring. That's what I always do; they leave off the sooner. Suddenly I heard a noise, a fuss and a bustle; I heard—did not my ears deceive me?—they were mentioning me, asking for me, calling Dyevushkin. My heart began shuddering within me, and I don't know myself why I was so frightened; I only know I was panic-stricken as I had never been before in my life. I sat rooted to my chair—as though there were nothing the matter, as though it were not I. But they began getting nearer and nearer. And at last, close to my ear, they were calling, "Dyevushkin, Dyevushkin! Where is Dyevushkin?" I raised my eyes: Yevstafy Ivanovitch stood before me; he said: "Makar Alexyevitch, make haste to his Excellency! You've made a mistake in that document!" That was all he said, but it was enough; enough had been said, hadn't it, Varinka? Half dead, frozen with terror, not knowing what I was doing, I went—why, I was more dead than alive. I was led through one room, through a second, through a third, to his Excellency's study. I was in his presence! I can give you no exact account of what my thoughts were then. I saw his Excellency standing up, they were all standing round him. I believe I did not bow, I forgot. I was so flustered that my lips were trembling, my legs were trembling. And I had reason to be, my dear girl! To begin with, I was ashamed; I glanced into the looking-glass on the right hand and what I saw there was enough to send one out of one's mind. And in the second place, I had always tried to behave as if there were no such person in the world. So that his Excellency could hardly have been aware of my existence. Perhaps he may have heard casually that there was a clerk called Dyevushkin in the office, but he had never gone into the matter more closely.

He began, angrily: "What were you about, sir? Where were your eyes? The copy was wanted; it was wanted in a hurry, and you spoil it."

At this point, his Excellency turned to Yevstafy Ivanovitch. I could only catch a word here and there: "Negligence! Carelessness! You will get us into difficulties!" I would have opened my mouth to say something. I wanted to beg for forgiveness, but I could not; I wanted to run away, but dared not attempt it, and then . . . then, Varinka, something happened so awful that I can hardly hold my pen, for shame, even now. A button—the devil take the button—which was hanging by a thread on my uniform—suddenly flew off, bounced on the floor (I must have caught hold of it accidentally) with a jingle, the damned thing, and rolled straight to his Excellency's feet, and that in the midst of a profound silence! And that was my only justification, my sole apology, my only answer, all that I had to say to his Excellency! What followed was awful. His Excellency's attention was at once turned to my appearance and my attire. I remembered what I had seen in the looking-glass; I flew to catch the button! Some idiocy possessed me! I bent down, I tried to pick up the button—it twirled and rolled, I couldn't pick it up—in fact, I distinguished myself by my agility. Then I felt that my last faculties were deserting me, that everything, everything was lost, my whole reputation was lost, my dignity as a man was lost, and then, apropos of nothing, I had the voices of Teresa and Faldoni ringing in my ears. At last I picked up the button, stood up and drew myself erect, and if I were a fool I might at least have stood quietly with my hands at my sides! But not a bit of it. I began fitting the button to the torn threads as though it might hang on, and I actually smiled, actually smiled. His Excellency turned away at first, then he glanced at me again—I heard him say to Yevstafy Ivanovitch: "How is this? . . . Look at him! . . . What is he? . . . What sort of man? . . ." Ah, my own, think of that! "What is he?" and, "what sort of man?" I had distinguished myself! I heard Yevstafy Ivanovitch say: "No note against him, no note against him for anything, behaviour excellent, salary in accordance with his grade . . ." "Well, assist him in some way, let him have something in advance," says his Excellency. . . . "But he has had an advance," he said; "he has had his salary in advance for such and such a time. He is apparently in difficulties, but his conduct is good, and there is no note, there never has been a note against him."

My angel, I was burning, burning in the fires of hell! I was dying. . . .

"Well," said his Excellency, "make haste and copy it again; Dyevushkin, come here, copy it over again without a mistake; and listen . . ." Here his Excellency turned to the others, gave them various instructions and they all went away. As soon as they had gone, his Excellency hurriedly took out his notebook and from it took a hundred-rouble note. "Here," said he, "take it as you like, so far as I can help you, take it . . ." and he thrust it into my hand. I trembled, my angel, my whole soul was quivering; I don't know what happened to me, I tried to seize his hand to kiss it, but he flushed crimson, my darling, and—here I am not departing one hair's breadth from the truth, my own—he took my unworthy hand and shook it, just took it and shook it, as though I had been his equal, as though I had been just such a General as himself. "You can go," he said; "whatever I can do for you . . . don't make mistakes, but there, no great harm done this time."

Now Varinka, this is what I have decided. I beg you and Fedora, and if I had any children I should bid them, to pray every day and all our lives for his Excellency as they would not pray for their own father! I will say more, my dear, and I say it solemnly—pay attention, Varinka—I swear that however cast down I was and afflicted in the bitterest days of our misfortunes, looking at you, at your poverty, and at myself, my degradation and my uselessness, in spite of all that, I swear that the hundred roubles is not as much to me as that his Excellency deigned to shake hands with me, a straw, a worthless drunkard! By that he has restored me to myself, by that action he has lifted up my spirit, has made my life sweeter for ever, and I am firmly persuaded that, however sinful I may be before the Almighty, yet my prayers for the happiness and prosperity of his Excellency will reach His Throne! . . .

My darling! I am dreadfully upset, dreadfully excited now, my heart is beating as though it would burst out of my breast, and I feel, as it were, weak all over.

I am sending you forty-five roubles; I am giving the landlady twenty and leaving thirty-five for myself. For twenty I can put my wardrobe in order, and I shall have fifteen left to go on with. But just now all the impressions of the morning have shaken my whole being, I am going to lie down. I am at peace, quite at peace, though; only there is an ache in my heart and deep down within me I feel my soul quivering, trembling, stirring.

I am coming to see you: but now I am simply drunk with all these sensations. . . . God sees all, my Varinka, my priceless darling!

Your worthy friend,
MAKAR DYEVUSHKIN.

September 10.

MY DEAR MAKAR ALEXYEVITCH,

I am unutterably delighted at your happiness and fully appreciate the goodness of your chief, my friend. So now you will have a little respite from trouble! But, for God's sake, don't waste your money again. Live quietly and as frugally as possible, and from to-day begin to put by a little that misfortune may not find you unprepared again. For goodness' sake don't worry about us. Fedora and I will get along somehow. Why have you sent us so much money, Makar Alexyevitch? We don't need it at all. We are satisfied with what we have. It is true we shall soon want money for moving from this lodging, but Fedora is hoping to be repaid an old debt that has been owing for years. I will keep twenty roubles, however, in case of extreme necessity. The rest I send you back. Please take care of your money, Makar Alexyevitch. Good-bye. Be at peace now, keep well and happy. I would write more to you, but I feel dreadfully tired; yesterday I did not get up all day. You do well to promise to come. Do come and see me, please, Makar Alexyevitch.

V. D.

September 11.

MY DEAR VARVARA ALEXYEVNA,

I beseech you, my own, not to part from me now, now when I am quite happy and contented with everything. My darling! Don't listen to Fedora and I will do anything you like; I shall behave well if only from respect to his Excellency. I will behave well and carefully; we will write to each other happy letters again, we will confide in each other our thoughts, our joys, our cares, if we have any cares; we will live together in happiness and concord. We'll study literature . . . My angel! My whole fate has changed and everything has changed for the better.

The landlady has become more amenable. Teresa is more sensible, even Faldoni has become prompter. I have made it up with Ratazyaev. In my joy I went to him of myself. He's really a good fellow, Varinka, and all the harm that was said of him was nonsense. I have discovered that it was all an abominable slander. He had no idea whatever of describing us. He read me a new work of his. And as for his calling me a Lovelace, that was not an insulting or abusive name; he explained it to me. The word is taken straight from a foreign source and means *a clever fellow,* and to express it more elegantly, in a literary fashion, it means a young man you must be on the lookout with, you see, and nothing of that sort. It was an innocent jest, my angel! I'm an ignoramus and in my foolishness I was offended. In fact, it is I who apologised to him now. . . . And the weather is so wonderful to-day, Varinka, so fine. It is true there was a slight frost this morning, as though it had been sifted through a sieve. It was nothing. It only made the air a little fresher. I went to buy some boots, and I bought some wonderful boots. I walked along the Nevsky. I read the *Bee.* Why! I am forgetting to tell you the principal thing.

It was this, do you see.

This morning I talked to Emelyan Ivanovitch and to Axentey Mihalovitch about his Excellency. Yes, Varinka, I'm not the only one he has treated to graciously. I am not the only one he has befriended, and he is known to all the world for the goodness of his heart. His praises are sung in very many quarters, and tears of gratitude are shed. An orphan girl was brought up in his house. He gave her a dowry and married her to a man in a good position, to a clerk on special commissions, who was in attendance on his Excellency. He installed a son of a widow in some office, and has done a great many other acts of kindness. I thought it my duty at that point to add my mite and described his Excellency's action in the hearing of all; I told them all and concealed nothing. I put my pride in my pocket, as though pride or dignity mattered in a case like that. So I told it aloud—to do glory to the good deeds of his Excellency! I spoke enthusiastically, I spoke with warmth, I did not blush, on the contrary, I was proud that I had such a story to tell. I told them about everything (only I was judiciously silent about you, Varinka), about my landlady, about Faldoni, about Ratazyaev, about my boots and about Markov—I told them everything. Some of them laughed a little, in fact, they all laughed a little. Probably they found something funny in my appearance, or it may have been about my boots—yes, it must have been about my boots. They could not have done it with any bad intention. It was nothing, just youthfulness, or perhaps because they are well-to-do people, but they could not jeer at what I said with any bad, evil intention. That is, what I said about his Excellency—that they could not do. Could they, Varinka?

I still can't get over it, my darling. The whole incident has so over-whelmed me! Have you got any firewood? Don't catch cold, Varinka; you can so easily catch cold. Ah, my own precious, you crush me with your sad thoughts. I pray to God, how I pray to Him for you, my dearie! For instance, have you got woollen stockings, and other warm underclothing? Mind, my darling, if you need anything, for God's sake don't wound your old friend, come straight to me. Now our bad times are over. Don't be anxious about me. Everything is so bright, so happy in the future!

It was a sad time, Varinka! But there, no matter, it's past! Years will pass and we shall sigh for that time. I remember my young days. Why, I often hadn't a farthing! I was cold and hungry, but light-hearted, that was all. In the morning I would walk along the Nevsky, see a pretty little face and be happy all day. It was a splendid, splendid time, my darling! It is nice to be alive, Varinka! Especially in Petersburg. I repented with tears in my eyes yesterday, and prayed to the Lord God to forgive me all my sins in that sad time: my repining, my liberal ideas, my drinking and despair. I remembered you with emotion in my prayers. You were my only support, Varinka, you were my only comfort, you cheered me on my way with counsel and good advice. I can never forget that, dear one. I have kissed all your letters to-day, my darling! Well, good-bye, my precious. They say that somewhere near here there is a sale of clothing. So I will make inquiries a little. Good-bye, my angel. Good-bye!

> Your deeply devoted,
> MAKAR DYEVUSHKIN.

September 15.

DEAR MAKAR ALEXYEVITCH,

I feel dreadfully upset. Listen what has happened here. I foresee something momentous. Judge yourself, my precious friend; Mr. Bykov is in Petersburg, Fedora met him. He was driving, he ordered the cab to stop, went up to Fedora himself and began asking where she was living. At first she would not tell him. Then he said, laughing, that he knew who was living with her. (Evidently Anna Fyodorovna had told him all about it.) Then Fedora could not contain herself and began upbraiding him on the spot, in the street, reproaching him, telling him he was an immoral man and the cause of all my troubles. He answered, that one who has not a halfpenny is bound to have misfortunes. Fedora answered that I might have been able to earn my own living, that I might have been married or else have had some situation, but that now my happiness was wrecked for ever and that I was ill besides, and would not live long. To this he answered that I was still young, that I had still a lot of nonsense in my head and that my virtues were getting a little tarnished (his words). Fedora and I thought he did not know our lodging when suddenly, yesterday, just after I had gone out to buy some things in the Gostiny Dvor he walked into our room. I believe he did not want to find me at home. He questioned Fedora at length concerning our manner of life, examined everything we had; he looked at my work; at last asked, "Who is this clerk you have made friends with?" At that moment you walked across the yard; Fedora pointed to you; he glanced and laughed; Fedora begged him to go away, told him that I was unwell, as it was, from grieving, and that to see him in our room would be very distasteful to me. He was silent for a while; said that he had just looked in with no object and tried to give Fedora twenty-five roubles; she, of course, did not take it.

What can it mean? What has he come to see us for? I cannot understand where he has found out all about us! I am lost in conjecture. Fedora says that Axinya, her sister-in-law, who comes to see us, is friendly with Nastasya the laundress, and Nastasya's cousin is a porter in the office in which a friend of Anna Fyodorovna's nephew is serving. So has not, perhaps, some ill-natured gossip crept round? But it is very possible that Fedora is mistaken; we don't know what to think. Is it possible he will come to us again! The mere thought of it terrifies me! When Fedora told me all about it yesterday, I was so frightened that I almost fainted with terror! What more does he want? I don't want to know him now! What does he want with me, poor me? Oh! I am in such terror now, I keep expecting Bykov to walk in every minute. What will happen to me, what more has fate in store for me? For Christ's sake, come and see me now, Makar Alexyevitch. Do come, for God's sake, come.

September 18.

My darling Varvara Alexyevna!

To-day an unutterably sad, quite unaccountable and unexpected event has occurred here. Our poor Gorshkov (I must tell you, Varinka) has had his character completely cleared. The case was concluded some time ago and to-day he went to hear the final judgment. The case ended very happily for him. He was fully exonerated of any blame for negligence and carelessness. The merchant was condemned to pay him a considerable sum of money, so that his financial position was vastly improved and no stain left on his honour and things were better all round—in fact, he won everything he could have desired.

He came home at three o'clock this afternoon. He did not look like himself, his face was white as a sheet, his lips quivered and he kept smiling—he embraced his wife and children. We all flocked to congratulate him. He was greatly touched by our action, he bowed in all directions, shook hands with all of us several times. It even seemed to me as though he were taller and more erect, and no longer had that running tear in his eye. He was in such excitement, poor fellow. He could not stand still for two minutes: he picked up anything he came across, then dropped it again; and kept continually smiling and bowing, sitting down, getting up and sitting down again. Goodness knows what he said: "My honour, my honour, my good name, my children," and that was how he kept talking! He even shed tears. Most of us were moved to tears, too; Ratazyaev clearly wanted to cheer him up, and said, "What is honour, old man, when one has nothing to eat? The money, the money's the thing, old man, thank God for that!" and thereupon he slapped him on the shoulder. It seemed to me that Gorshkov was offended—not that he openly showed dissatisfaction, but he looked rather strangely at Ratazyaev and took his hand off his shoulder. And that had never happened before, Varinka! But characters differ. Now I, for instance, should not have stood on my dignity, at a time of such joy; why, my own, sometimes one is too liberal with one's bows and almost cringing from nothing but excess of good-nature and soft-heartedness. . . . However, no matter about me!

"Yes," he said, "the money is a good thing too, thank God, thank God!" And then all the time we were with him he kept repeating, "Thank God, thank God."

His wife ordered a rather nice and more ample dinner. Our landlady cooked for them herself. Our landlady is a good-natured woman in a way. And until dinner-time Gorshkov could not sit still in his seat. He went into the lodgers' rooms, without waiting to be invited. He just went in, smiled, sat down on the edge of a chair, said a word or two, or even said nothing, and went away again. At the naval man's he even took a hand at cards; they made up a game with him as fourth. He played a little, made a muddle of it, played three or four rounds and threw down the cards. "No," he said, "you see, I just looked in, I just looked in," and he went away from them. He met me in the passage, took both my hands, looked me straight in the face, but so strangely; then shook hands with me and walked away, and kept smiling, but with a strange, painful smile like a dead man. His wife was crying with joy; everything was cheerful as though it were a holiday. They soon had dinner. After dinner he said to his wife: "I tell you what, my love, I'll lie down a little," and he went to his bed. He called his little girl, put his hand on her head, and for a long time he was stroking the child's head. Then he turned to his wife again, "And what of Petinka? our Petya!" he said. "Petinka?" . . . His wife crossed herself and answered that he was dead. "Yes, yes, I know all about it. Petinka is now in the Kingdom of Heaven." His wife saw that he was not himself, that what had happened had completely upset him, and she said to him, "You ought to have a nap, my love." "Yes, very well, I will directly . . . just a little," then he turned away, lay still for a bit, then turned round, tried to say something. His wife could not make out what he said, and asked him, "What is it, my dear?" and he did not answer. She waited a little, "Well, he's asleep," she thought, and went into the landlady's for an hour. An hour later she came back, she saw her husband had not woken up and was not stirring. She thought he was asleep, and she sat down and began working at something. She said that for half an hour she was so lost in musing that she did not know what she was thinking about, all she can say is that she did not think of her husband. But suddenly she was roused by the feeling of uneasiness, and what struck her first of all was the death-like silence in the room. . . . She looked at the bed and saw that her husband was lying in the same position. She went up to him, pulled down the quilt and looked at him—and he was already cold—he was dead, my darling. Gorshkov was dead, he had died suddenly, as though he had been killed by a thunder-bolt. And why he died, God only knows. It was such a shock to me, Varinka, that I can't get over it now. One can't believe that a man could die so easily. He was such a poor, unlucky fellow, that Gorshkov! And what a fate, what a fate! His wife was in tears and panic-stricken. The little girl crept away into a corner. There is such a hubbub going on, they will hold a post-mortem and inquest . . . I can't tell you just what. But the pity of it, oh, the pity of it! It's sad to think that in reality one does not know the day or the hour . . . One dies so easily for no reason . . .

Your
MAKAR DYEVUSHKIN.

September 19.

DEAR VARVARA ALEXYEVNA,

I hasten to inform you, my dear, that Ratazyaev has found me work with a writer. Someone came to him, and brought him such a fat manuscript—thank God, a lot of work. But it's so illegibly written that I don't know how to set to work on it: they want it in a hurry. It's all written in such a way that one does not understand it. . . . They have agreed to pay forty kopecks the sixteen pages. I write you all this, my own, because now I shall have extra money. And now, good-bye, my darling, I have come straight from work.

Your faithful friend,
MAKAR DYEVUSHKIN.

September 23.

MY DEAR FRIEND, MAKAR ALEXYEVITCH,

For three days I have not written you a word, and I have had a great many anxieties and worries.

The day before yesterday Bykov was here. I was alone, Fedora had gone off somewhere. I opened the door to him, and was so frightened when I saw him that I could not move. I felt that I turned pale. He walked in as he always does, with a loud laugh, took a chair and sat down. For a long while I could not recover myself. At last I sat down in the corner to my work. He even left off laughing. I believe my appearance impressed him. I have grown so thin of late, my eyes and my cheeks are hollow, I was as white as a sheet . . . it would really be hard for anyone to recognise me who had known me a year ago. He looked long and intently at me; then at last he began to be lively again, said something or other; I don't know what I answered, and he laughed again. He stayed a whole hour with me; talked to me a long time; asked me some questions. At last just before leaving, he took me by the hand and said (I write you it word for word): "Varvara Alexyevitch, between ourselves, be it said, your relation and my intimate friend, Anna Fyodorovna, is a very nasty woman" (then he used an unseemly word about her). "She led your cousin astray, and ruined you. I behaved like a rascal in that case, too; but after all, it's a thing that happens every day." Then he laughed heartily. Then he observed that he was not great at fine speeches, and that most of what he had to explain, about which the obligations of gentlemanly feeling forbade him to be silent, he had told me already, and that in brief words he would come to the rest. Then he told me he was asking my hand in marriage, that he thought it his duty to restore my good name, that he was rich, that after the wedding he would take me away to his estates in the steppes, that he wanted to go coursing hares there; that he would never come back to Petersburg again, because it was horrid in Petersburg; that he had here in Petersburg—as he expressed it—a good-for-nothing nephew whom he had sworn to deprive of the estate, and it was just for that reason in the hope of having legitimate heirs that he sought my hand, that it was the chief cause of his courtship. Then he observed that I was living in a very poor way: and it was no wonder I was ill living in such a slum; predicted that I should certainly die if I stayed there another month; said that lodgings in Petersburg were horrid, and finally asked me if I wanted anything.

I was so overcome at his offer that, I don't know why, I began crying. He took my tears for gratitude and told me he had always been sure I was a good, feeling, and educated girl, but that he had not been able to make up his mind to take this step till he had found out about my present behaviour in full detail. Then he asked me about you, said that he had heard all about it, that you were a man of good principles, that he did not want to be indebted to you and asked whether five hundred roubles would be enough for all that you had done for me. When I explained to him that what you had done for me no money could repay, he said that it was all nonsense, that that was all romantic stuff out of novels, that I was young and read poetry, that novels were the ruin of young girls, that books were destructive of morality and that he could not bear books of any sort, he advised me to wait till I was his age and then talk about people. "Then," he added, "you will know what men are like." Then he said I was to think over his offer thoroughly, that he would very much dislike it if I were to take such an important step thoughtlessly; he added that thoughtlessness and impulsiveness were the ruin of inexperienced youth, but that he quite hoped for a favourable answer from me, but that in the opposite event, he should be forced to marry some Moscow shopkeeper's daughter, "because," he said, "I have sworn that good-for-nothing nephew shall not have the estate."

He forced five hundred roubles into my hands, as he said, "to buy sweetmeats." He said that in the country I should grow as round as a bun, that with him I should be living on the fat of the land, that he had a terrible number of things to see to now, that he was dragging about all day on business, and that he had just slipped in to see me between his engagements. Then he went away.

I thought for a long time, I pondered many things, I wore myself out thinking, my friend; at last I made up my mind. My friend, I shall marry him. I ought to accept his offer. If anyone can rescue me from my shame, restore my good name, and ward off poverty, privation and misfortune from me in the future, it is he and no one else. What more can one expect from the future, what more can one expect from fate? Fedora says I must not throw away my good fortune; she says, if this isn't good fortune, what is? Anyway, I can find no other course for me, my precious friend. What am I to do? I have ruined my health with work as it is; I can't go on working continually. Go into a family? I should pine away with depression, besides I should be of no use to anyone. I am of a sickly constitution, and so I shall always be a burden on other people. Of course I am not going into a paradise, but what am I to do, my friend, what am I to do? What choice have I?

I have not asked your advice. I wanted to think it over alone. The decision you have just read is unalterable, and I shall immediately inform Bykov of it, he is pressing me to answer quickly. He said that his business would not wait, that he must be off, and that he couldn't put it off for nonsense. God knows whether I shall be happy, my fate is in His holy, inscrutable power, but I have made up my mind. They say Bykov is a kind-hearted man: he will respect me; perhaps I, too, shall respect him. What more can one expect from such a marriage?

I will let you know about everything, Makar Alexyevitch. I am sure you will understand all my wretchedness. Do not try to dissuade me from my intention. Your efforts will be in vain. Weigh in your own mind all that has forced me to this step. I was very much distressed at first, but now I am calmer. What is before me, I don't know. What will be, will be; as God wills! . . .

Bykov has come, I leave this letter unfinished. I wanted to tell you a great deal more. Bykov is here already!

September 23.

My darling Varvara Alexyevna,

I hasten to answer you, my dear; I hasten to tell you, my precious, that I am dumbfounded. It all seems so . . . Yesterday we buried Gorshkov. Yes, that is so, Varinka, that is so; Bykov has behaved honourably; only, you see, my own . . . so you have consented. Of course, everything is according to God's will; that is so, that certainly must be so—that is, it certainly must be God's will in this; and the providence of the Heavenly Creator is blessed, of course, and inscrutable, and it is fate too, and they are the same. Fedora sympathises with you too. Of course you will be happy now, my precious, you will live in comfort, my darling, my little dearie, little angel and light of my eyes—only Varinka, how can it be so soon? . . . Yes, business. . . . Mr. Bykov has business—of course, everyone has business, and he may have it too. . . . I saw him as he came out from you. He's a good-looking man, good-looking; a very good-looking man, in fact. Only there is something queer about it, the point is not whether he is a good-looking man. Indeed, I am not myself at all. Why, how are we to go on writing to one another? I . . . I shall be left alone. I am weighing everything, my angel, I am weighing everything as you write to me, I am weighing it all in my heart, the reasons. I had just finished copying the twentieth quire, and meanwhile these events have come upon us! Here you are going on a journey, my darling, you will have to buy all sorts of things, shoes of all kinds, a dress, and I know just the shop in Gorohovoy Street; do you remember how I described it to you? But no! How can you, Varinka? what are you about? You can't go away now, it's quite impossible, utterly impossible. Why, you will have to buy a great many things and get a carriage. Besides, the weather is so awful now; look, the rain is coming down in bucketfuls, and such soaking rain, too, and what's more . . . what's more, you will be cold, my angel; your little heart will be cold! Why, you are afraid of anyone strange, and yet you go. And to whom am I left, all alone here? Yes! Here, Fedora says that there is great happiness in store for you . . . but you know she's a headstrong woman, she wants to be the death of me. Are you going to the evening service to-night, Varinka? I would go to have a look at you. It's true, perfectly true, my darling, that you are a well-educated, virtuous and feeling girl, only he had much better marry the shopkeeper's daughter! Don't you think so, my precious? He had better marry the shopkeeper's daughter! I will come to see you, Varinka, as soon as it gets dark, I shall just run in for an hour. It will get dark early to-day, then I shall run in. I shall certainly come to you for an hour this evening, my darling. Now you are expecting Bykov, but when he goes, then . . . Wait a bit, Varinka, I shall run across . . .

MAKAR DYEVUSHKIN.

September 27.

MY DEAR FRIEND, MAKAR ALEXYEVITCH,

Mr. Bykov says I must have three dozen linen chemises. So I must make haste and find seamstresses to make two dozen, and we have very little time. Mr. Bykov is angry and says there is a great deal of bother over these rags. Our wedding is to be in five days, and we are to set off the day after the wedding. Mr. Bykov is in a hurry, he says we must not waste much time over nonsense. I am worn out with all this fuss and can hardly stand on my feet. There is a terrible lot to do, and perhaps it would have been better if all this had not happened. Another thing: we have not enough net or lace, so we ought to buy some more, for Mr. Bykov says he does not want his wife to go about like a cook, and that I simply must "wipe all the country ladies' noses for them." That was his own expression. So, Makar Alexyevitch, please apply to Madame Chiffon in Gorohovoy Street, and ask her first to send us some seamstresses, and secondly, to be so good as to come herself. I am ill to-day. It's so cold in our new lodging and the disorder is terrible. Mr. Bykov's aunt can scarcely breathe, she is so old. I am afraid she may die before we set off, but Mr. Bykov says that it is nothing, she'll wake up. Everything in the house is in the most awful confusion. Mr. Bykov is not living with us, so the servants are racing about in all directions, goodness knows where. Sometimes Fedora is the only one to wait on us, and Mr. Bykov's valet, who looks after everything, has disappeared no one knows where for the last three days. Mr. Bykov comes to see us every morning, and yesterday he beat the superintendent of the house, for which he got into trouble with the police. I have not even had anyone to take my letters to you. I am writing by post. Yes! I had almost forgotten the most important point. Tell Madame Chiffon to be sure and change the net, matching it with the pattern she had yesterday, and to come to me herself to show the new, and tell her, too, that I have changed my mind about the embroidery, that it must be done in crochet; and another thing, that the letters for the monogram on the handkerchiefs must be done in tambour stitch, do you hear? Tambour stitch and not satin stitch. Mind you don't forget that it is to be tambour stitch! Something else I had almost forgotten! For God's sake tell her also that the leaves on the pelerine are to be raised and that the tendrils and thorns are to be in appliqué; and, then, the collar is to be edged with lace, or a deep frill. Please tell her, Makar Alexyevitch.

Your

V. D.

P. S.—I am so ashamed of worrying you with all my errands. The day before yesterday you were running about all the morning. But what can I do! There's no sort of order in the house here, and I am not well. So don't be vexed with me, Makar Alexyevitch. I'm so miserable. Oh, how will it end, my friend, my dear, my kind Makar Alexyevitch? I'm afraid to look into my future. I have a presentiment of something and am living in a sort of delirium.

P.P.S.—For God's sake, my friend, don't forget anything of what I have told you. I am so afraid you will make a mistake. Remember tambour, not satin stitch.

V. D.

September 27.

DEAR VARVARA ALEXYEVNA,

I have carried out all your commissions carefully. Madame Chiffon says that she had thought herself of doing them in tambour stitch; that it is more correct, or something, I don't know, I didn't take it in properly. And you wrote about a frill, too, and she talked about the frill.

Only I have forgotten, my darling, what she told me about the frill. All that I remember is, that she said a great deal; such a horrid woman! What on earth was it? But she will tell you about it herself. I have become quite dissipated, Varinka, I have not even been to the office to-day. But there's no need for you to be in despair about that, my own. I am ready to go the round of all the shops for your peace of mind. You say you are afraid to look into the future. But at seven o'clock this evening you will know all about it. Madame Chiffon is coming to see you herself. So don't be in despair; you must hope for the best, everything will turn out for the best—so there. Well, now, I keep thinking about that cursed frill—ugh! bother that frill! I should have run round to you, my angel, I should have looked in, I should certainly have looked in; I have been to the gates of your house, once or twice. But Bykov—that is, I mean, Mr. Bykov—is always so cross, you see it doesn't . . . Well, what of it!

MAKAR DYEVUSHKIN.

September 28.

MY DEAR MAKAR ALEXYEVITCH,

For God's sake, run at once to the jeweller's: tell him that he must not make the pearl and emerald ear-rings. Mr. Bykov says that it is too gorgeous, that it's too expensive. He is angry; he says, that as it is, it is costing him a pretty penny, and we are robbing him, and yesterday he said that if he had known beforehand and had any notion of the expense he would not have bound himself. He says that as soon as we are married we will set off at once, that we shall have no visitors and that I needn't hope for dancing and flirtation, and that the holidays are a long way off. That's how he talks. And, God knows, I don't want anything of that sort! Mr. Bykov ordered everything himself. I don't dare to answer him: he is so hasty. What will become of me?

V. D.

September 28.

MY DARLING VARVARA ALEXYEVNA,

I—that is, the jeweller said—very good; and I meant to say at first that I have been taken ill and cannot get up. Here now, at such an urgent, busy time I have caught a cold, the devil take it! I must tell you, to complete my misfortunes, his Excellency was pleased to be stern and was very angry with Emelyan Ivanovitch and scolded him, and he was quite worn out at last, poor man. You see, I tell you about everything. I wanted to write to you about something else, but I am afraid to trouble you. You see, I am a foolish, simple man, Varinka, I just write what comes, so that, maybe, you may—— But there, never mind!

Your

MAKAR DYEVUSHKIN.

September 29.

VARVARA ALEXYEVITCH, MY OWN,

I saw Fedora to-day, my darling, she says that you are to be married to-morrow, and that the day after you are setting off, and that Mr. Bykov is engaging horses already. I have told you about his Excellency already, my darling. Another thing—I have checked the bills from the shop in Gorohovoy; it is all correct, only the things are very dear. But why is Mr. Bykov angry with you? Well, may you be happy, Varinka! I am glad, yes, I shall be glad if you are happy. I should come to the church, my dear, but I've got lumbago. So I keep on about our letters; who will carry them for us, my precious? Yes! You have been a good friend to Fedora, my own! You have done a good deed, my dear, you have done quite right. It's a good deed! And God will bless you for every good deed. Good deeds never go unrewarded, and virtue will sooner or later be rewarded by the eternal justice of God. Varinka! I wanted to write to you a great deal; I could go on writing and writing every minute, every hour! I have one of your books still, *Byelkin's Stories.* I tell you what, Varinka, don't take it away, make me a present of it, my darling. It is not so much that I want to read it. But you know yourself, my darling, winter is coming on: the evenings will be long; it will be sad, and then I could read. I shall move from my lodgings, Varinka, into your old room and lodge with Fedora. I would not part from that honest woman for anything now; besides, she is such a hard-working woman. I looked at your empty room carefully yesterday. Your embroidery frame has remained untouched, just as it was with embroidery on it. I examined your needlework; there were all sorts of little scraps left there, you had begun winding thread on one of my letters. On the little table I found a piece of paper with the words "Dear Makar Alexyevitch, I hasten—" and that was all. Someone must have interrupted you at the most interesting place. In the corner behind the screen stands your little bed. . . . Oh, my darling!!! Well, good-bye, good-bye, send me some answer to this letter quickly.

MAKAR DYEVUSHKIN.

September 30.

MY PRECIOUS FRIEND, MAKAR ALEXYEVITCH,

Everything is over! My lot is cast; I don't know what it will be, but I am resigned to God's will. To-morrow we set off. I say good-bye to you for the last time, my precious one, my friend, my benefactor, my own! Don't grieve for me, live happily, think of me, and may God's blessing descend on us! I shall often remember you in my thoughts, in my prayers. So this time is over! I bring to my new life little consolation from the memories of the past; the more precious will be my memory of you, the more precious will your memory be to my heart. You are my one friend; you are the only one there who loved me. You know I have seen it all, I know how you love me! You were happy in a smile from me and a few words from my pen. Now you will have to get used to being without me. How will you do, left alone here? To whom am I leaving you my kind, precious, only friend! I leave you the book, the embroidery frame, the unfinished letter; when you look at those first words, you must read in your thoughts all that you would like to hear or read from me, all that I should have written to you; and what I could not write now! Think of your poor Varinka who loves you so truly. All your letters are at Fedora's in the top drawer of a chest. You write that you are ill and Mr. Bykov will not let me go out anywhere to-day. I will write to you, my friend, I promise; but, God alone knows what may happen. And so, we are saying good-bye now for ever, my friend, my darling, my own, for ever. . . . Oh, if only I could embrace you now! Good-bye, my dear; good-bye, good-bye. Live happily, keep well. My prayers will be always for you. Oh! how sad I am, how weighed down in my heart. Mr. Bykov is calling me.

Your ever loving

V.

P.S.—My soul is so full, so full of tears now . . . tears are choking me, rending my heart. Good-bye. Oh, God, how sad I am!

Remember me, remember your poor Varinka.

VARINKA, MY DARLING, MY PRECIOUS,

You are being carried off, you are going. They had better have torn the heart out of my breast than take you from me! How could you do it? Here you are weeping and going away! Here I have just had a letter from you, all smudged with tears. So you don't want to go; so you are being taken away by force; so you are sorry for me; so you love me! And with whom will you be now? Your little heart will be sad, sick and cold out there. It will be sapped by misery, torn by grief. You will die out there, they will put you in the damp earth; there will be no one to weep for you there! Mr. Bykov will be always coursing hares. Oh, my darling, my darling! What have you brought yourself to? How could you make up your mind to such a step? What have you done, what have you done, what have you done to yourself? They'll drive you to your grave out there; they will be the death of you, my angel. You know you are as weak as a little feather, my own! And where was I, old fool, where were my eyes! I saw the child did not know what she was doing, the child was simply in a fever! I ought simply—— But no, fool, fool, I thought nothing and saw nothing, as though that were the right thing, as though it had nothing to do with me; and went running after frills and flounces too. . . . No, Varinka, I shall get up; to-morrow, maybe, I shall be better and then I shall get up! . . . I'll throw myself under the wheels, my precious, I won't let you go away! Oh, no, how can it be? By what right is all this done? I will go with you; I will run after your carriage if you won't take me, and will run my hardest as long as there is a breath left in my body. And do you know what it is like where you are going, my darling? Maybe you don't know—if so, ask me! There it is, the steppe, my own, the steppe, the bare steppe; why, it is as bare as my hand; there, there are hard-hearted peasant women and uneducated drunken peasants. There the leaves are falling off the trees now, there it is cold and rainy—and you are going there! Well, Mr. Bykov has something to do there: he will be with hares; but what about you? Do you want to be a grand country lady, Varinka? But, my little cherub! you should just look at yourself. Do you look like a grand country lady? . . . Why, how can such a thing be, Varinka? To whom am I going to write letters, my darling? Yes! You must take that into consideration, my darling— you must ask yourself, to whom is he going to write letters? Whom am I to call my darling; whom am I to call by that loving name, where am I to find you afterwards, my angel? I shall die, Varinka, I shall certainly die; my heart will never survive such a calamity! I loved you like God's sunshine, I loved you like my own daughter, I loved everything in you, my darling, my own! And I lived only for you! I worked and copied papers, and walked and went about and put my thoughts down on paper, in friendly letters, all because you, my precious, were living here opposite, close by; perhaps you did not know it, but that was how it was. Yes, listen, Varinka; you only think, my sweet darling, how is it possible that you should go away from us? You can't go away, my own, it is impossible; it's simply utterly impossible! Why, it's raining, you are delicate, you will catch cold. Your carriage will be wet through; it will certainly get wet through. It won't get beyond the city gates before it will break down; it will break down on purpose. They make these carriages in Petersburg so badly: I know all those carriage makers; they are only fit to turn out a little model, a plaything, not anything solid. I'll take my oath they won't build it solid. I'll throw myself on my knees before Mr. Bykov: I will explain to him, I will explain everything, and you, my precious, explain to him, make him see reason! Tell him that you will stay and that you cannot go away! . . . Ah, why didn't he marry a shopkeeper's daughter in Moscow? He might just as well have married her! The shopkeeper's daughter would have suited him much better, she would have suited him much better. I know why! And I should have kept you here. What is he to you, my darling, what is Bykov? How has he suddenly become so dear to you? Perhaps it's because he is always buying frills and flounces. But what are frills and flounces? What good are frills and flounces? Why, it is nonsense, Varinka! Here it is a question of a man's life: and you know a frill's a rag; it's a rag, Varinka, a frill is; why, I shall buy you frills myself, that's all the reward I get; I shall buy them for you, my darling, I know a shop, that's all the reward you let me hope for, my cherub, Varinka. Oh Lord! Lord! So, you are really going to the steppes with Mr. Bykov, going away never to return! Ah, my darling! . . . No, you must write to me again, you must write another letter about everything, and when you go away you must write to me from there, or else, my heavenly angel, this will be the last letter and you know that this cannot be, this cannot be the last letter! Why, how can it be, so suddenly, actually the last? Oh no, I shall write and you will write. . . . Besides, I am acquiring a literary style. . . . Oh, my own, what does style matter, now? I don't know, now, what I am writing, I don't know at all, I don't know and I don't read it over and I don't improve the style. I write only to write, only to go on writing to you . . . my darling, my own, my Varinka. . . .